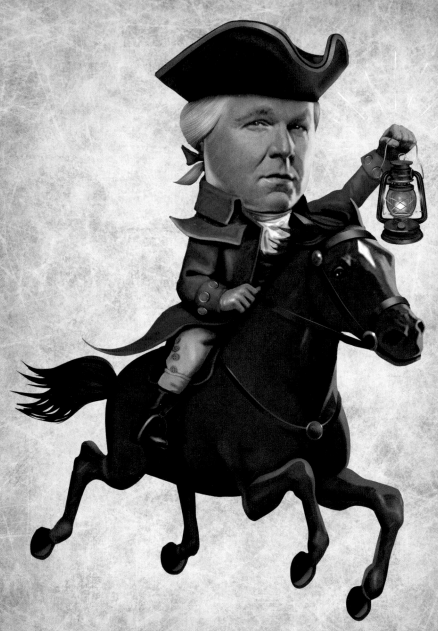

Shining the light on history

Rush Revere

and the

BRAVE PILGRIMS

Time-Travel Adventures with
Exceptional Americans

RUSH
LIMBAUGH

THRESHOLD EDITIONS

NEW YORK LONDON TORONTO SYDNEY NEW DELHI

Threshold Editions
A Division of Simon & Schuster, Inc.
1230 Avenue of the Americas
New York, NY 10020

First Threshold Editions hardcover edition October 2013

THRESHOLD EDITIONS and colophon are trademarks of Simon & Schuster, Inc.

For information about special discounts for bulk purchases,
please contact Simon & Schuster Special Sales at
1-866-506-1949 or business@simonandschuster.com.

The Simon & Schuster Speakers Bureau can bring authors to your live event.
For more information or to book an event, contact the Simon & Schuster Speakers
Bureau at 1-866-248-3049 or visit our website at www.simonspeakers.com.

Interior design by Ruth Lee-Mui

Manufactured in the United States of America

1 3 5 7 9 10 8 6 4 2

ISBN 978-1-4767-5586-1
ISBN 978-1-4767-5591-5 (ebook)

To Vince Flynn,
this book's Guardian Angel

KEY TO DRAWING:

1. Poop deck

2. Half deck

3. Upper deck

4. Forecastle

5. Main deck where most of the Pilgrims were housed

6. Crew's quarters

7. Large hold

8. Special cabins

9. Helmsman with the whipstaff controlling the tiller

10. Tiller room

11. Captain's cabin

12. Beak

13. Bowsprit

14. Foremast

15. Mainmast

16. Mizzen mast

crew as they would have been packed into

the 1620 crossing.

A Note from the Author

We live in the greatest country on earth, the United States of America. But what makes it so great? Why do some call the United States a miracle? How did we become such a tremendous country in such a short period of time? After all, the United States is less than 250 years old!

I want to try to help you understand what "American Exceptionalism" and greatness is all about. It does not mean that we Americans are better than anyone else. It does not mean that there is something uniquely different about us as human beings compared to other people in the world. It does not mean that we as a country have never faced problems of our own.

American Exceptionalism and greatness means that America is special because it is different from all other countries in history. It is a land built on true freedom and individual liberty and it defends both around the world. The role of the United States is to encourage individuals to be the best that they can be, to try to improve their lives, reach their goals, and make their dreams come true. In most parts of the world, dreams never become more than dreams. In the United States, they come true every day. There are so many stories of Americans who started with very little, yet dreamed big, worked very hard, and became extremely successful.

The sad reality is that since the beginning of time, most citizens of the world have not been free. For hundreds and thousands of years, many people in other civilizations and countries were servants to their kings, leaders, and government. It didn't matter how hard these people worked to improve their lives, because their lives were not their own. They often feared for their lives and could not get out from under a ruling class no matter how hard they tried. Many of these people lived and continue to live in extreme poverty, with no clean water, limited food, and none of the luxuries that we often take for granted. Many citizens in the world were punished, sometimes severely, for having their own ideas, beliefs, and hopes for a better future.

The United States of America is unique because it is the exception to all this. Our country is the first country *ever* to be founded on the principle that all human beings are created as *free* people. The Founders of this phenomenal country believed all people were born to be free as individuals. And so, they established a government and leadership that recognized and established this for the first time ever in the world! America is a place where the individual person serves himself and his family, not the king, or ruling class, or government. America is a place where you can think, believe, and express yourself as you want. You can dream as big as you can and nothing is holding you back.

This book on the Pilgrims is part of the great tale of how the United States of America came to be. The Pilgrims came to our shores more than a century and a half before our country was established in 1776, but their reasons for coming to the

"New World" helped to sow the seeds of our nation. The story of the Pilgrims and their arrival in the "New World" has been taught for hundreds of years and in that time the story has been tweaked and changed by people to the point that it is often misunderstood. I want you to know the real story. What really happened, who the Pilgrims really were, and what they did when they arrived.

Let me introduce you to my good buddy Rush Revere! Together, we are going to rush, rush, rush into history and the story of the Pilgrims!

Prologue

The sea was wide, cold, and blustery. The large wooden ship rocked hard against the rolling waves. I'd been on the *Mayflower* for only thirty minutes but already my head was leaning over the side just in case I had to "feed the fish." Water splashed up from the side of the hull and then rained down upon the deck.

"You there!" a voice shouted from nearby.

I turned around to see a sailor staring and pointing in my direction. He was a couple of inches taller than me. His shoulders were broad and his beard was black and scraggly with a thin scar above his cheek.

"That's right. I'm talking to you. Get your landlubber legs over here and below deck!"

Couldn't this sailor see that I was in no position to move, let alone walk across the ship when the deck felt like a washing machine with the spin cycle on extra high?

No, of course not. For starters, washing machines didn't

exist in the year 1620. I turned back toward the sea as another wave of nausea swelled inside me.

Maybe my decision to teleport aboard the *Mayflower* and journey with the Pilgrims hadn't been such a good idea after all. In fact, maybe now would be a good time to time-jump back to modern-day America and get some seasickness pills.

Yes, that's it. I could get the pills, stabilize my motion sickness, and then return before the ship reached the New World.

Suddenly, someone grabbed my arm and spun me around. I nearly jumped into the water when the large sailor shouted directly into my face!

"The whole lot of you makes me sick!" he said. "We should throw all you Saints overboard. What's your name!?"

Saints? This was not my first encounter with someone from the past. Although I was feeling extremely queasy, I tipped my hat and introduced myself while trying not to fall over. "I'm not a Saint or a Separatist. I'm Rush Revere," I said. "I'm a history teacher from the twenty-first century. I've come to—"

"The twenty-first century! Blimey! You're mad! The whole lot of you! You think I care if you make it to New England?" The sailor laughed as he pushed his face into mine and said, "I don't. In fact, I'd rather feed you to the sharks and be done with you."

His breath smelled foul, like rotten fish. I gagged and suddenly I vomited as the boat lurched to the side and sent me facefirst into the unsuspecting sailor. We tumbled to the deck and I rolled up against the railing. I sat up, realizing that I felt a great deal better. Unfortunately, I couldn't say the same thing about Stinky Fish Breath. He was covered from head to toe in my regurgitated lunch.

"Argh! You puked all over me! You piece of scum! I'll throw

you overboard!" He scrambled to his feet and charged at me like a bull targeting a matador.

My horse, Liberty, was aboard the *Mayflower*, somewhere. "*Liberty!*" I yelled, stumbling backward. "I could use a little help over here!"

Now look, I know what you're thinking. What's a horse doing on the deck of the *Mayflower* in the middle of a storm-tossed sea? Good question. The truth is, my Liberty is no ordinary horse.

The ship rocked back and forth as water surged again over its bow and crashed down on the deck as if a large waterfall had been turned on and off. The sailor was only a few feet away and closing fast. I scanned the length of the *Mayflower*, searching high and low. Another rush of water nearly swept me off my feet. I looked down to see a large fish flopping around. The boat rocked again and the fish slid right between the legs of the sailor.

Not a bad idea, I thought. Right before the sailor grabbed me, I dove headfirst through his legs. For a split second, I thought I was through and beyond his grasp. The sailor's beefy hand grabbed my leg, then my coat, then hoisted me up by my collar.

"I hope you can swim!" yelled Fish Breath.

From over his shoulder I finally spotted what I had been searching for.

"And I hope you can fly!" Liberty replied to him.

Oh, yes, Liberty can talk. I told you he wasn't an ordinary horse. Before the man could even turn around to see who had spoken, Liberty kicked his hind legs and sent the sailor sailing high into the air and then he fell into a web of nets.

"Perfect shot!" Liberty said.

"You appeared in the nick of time," I said, starting to feel sick again.

"Leaping to the *Mayflower* in the middle of a storm wasn't my idea!" Liberty said, speaking very fast. "Yes, I can leap to different times in American history, but I'm not a weatherman. And horses don't like boats. There's an awful lot of water surrounding us and this constant rocking back and forth, back and forth—it's making me hungry." Liberty turned his neck from side to side as if searching for the nearest feedbag. "Do you know where we can get some food around here?"

I slipped onto Liberty's saddle and said, "Please, let's not talk about food. Right now I need you to open the time portal."

"Back to the future?" Liberty grinned.

"Yes! Back to modern-day America, please. Just try not to leap us into a tornado!"

Liberty started galloping and yelled, "*Rush, rush, rushing from history!*"

A swirling circle of gold and purple appeared on the deck of the *Mayflower*. As it grew bigger, Liberty bolted for the center and jumped through.

We were back in modern-day America.

Chapter 1

The school bell rang and a few more students rushed into the classroom followed by Principal Sherman. The principal of Manchester Middle School was not a small man. If the door frame were any smaller, the principal would have to duck his head and twist his way into the classroom. I stood outside in the hallway as the door closed but watched and heard what was happening through the door's small window.

"Attention, everyone, please take your seats," said the principal with authority. He stood at the front of the classroom, hands at his sides, while his eyes scanned the desks and chairs. "I have an important announcement."

The room went silent. It was apparent that Principal Sherman did not tolerate disrespect. "I have some unfortunate news," he said. "Your teacher, Ms. Borrington, needed some extra time away from the academy to help care for a sick family member. In the meantime, I feel very fortunate to have found such a qualified replacement. You know that at Manchester Middle School we have the smartest and most educated teachers. It is my pleasure to introduce you to your substitute, Mr. Revere."

As if on cue, I opened the door to the classroom and walked in. As Principal Sherman prattled on about the importance of giving me their whole attention, I walked over to the chalkboard and grabbed a piece of chalk. In the upper left corner I wrote my name.

R-U-S-H R-E-V-E-R-E.

Principal Sherman then turned to me and said, "Mr. Revere, the students of Manchester's honors history class are now in your charge. I kno-o-o-ow," he said, turning to the class and then back to me, "they will give you their utmost respect." While he walked past me on his way to the door he lowered his head and whispered, "If the boy in the back row with the red baseball cap gives you any trouble, please send him to my office." Without another word, he opened the door and disappeared.

As I turned to the students, I noticed a hand in the air from a girl with blond hair and two perfectly placed pink bows. Before I had a chance to even call on her she asked, "Your first name is 'Rush'? That's weird. And why are you dressed like . . . that?!" she said.

I could tell that this student was all business. If there were a pecking order in this class, she would probably be at the top of the food chain. I looked at my seating chart and replied, "Thank you, Elizabeth. Do you go by Liz?"

She rolled her eyes and nearly grunted, "No, unlike some people, I have a real name. It's Elizabeth."

"It's a lovely name, if you like four syllables" I said, winking.

"If you must know, my real name is Rusty. But when I was your age, my favorite class was history. In fact, I found myself rushing to history class every day I had it. I would rush from my home, rush down the street, rush through the school until I was sitting at my desk. Eventually, my teacher started calling me 'Rush' and it stuck."

Two girls leaned over and whispered to each other. One pointed at my pants and giggled. Ah, yes, my clothing! Certainly, my colonial shirt with a waistcoat and an outer coat over it, as well as knickers, stockings, and a three-cornered hat, was enough to make me look like I was ready to go trick-or-treating.

"You're probably wondering about my clothing," I said. "Can anyone guess who I'm dressed as?"

A couple of students raised their hands and I pointed to each one.

"George Washington?" said the first.

"Good guess, but no. However, I am dressed as someone who fought in the same revolutionary war as George Washington and they assuredly knew each other."

"Are you Thomas Jefferson?" asked another student.

"No, however, another good guess. Mr. Jefferson lived during the same time, but I don't think he could ride on a horse fast enough as if he was flying from city to city."

Then the boy with the red baseball cap raised his hand. He was smirking at me, the kind of look you give with the intent of hitting the bull's-eye on a dunking machine. Reluctantly, I pointed to him.

"Then you must be Peter Pan," he said.

The students burst out laughing, and now I understood the warning from Principal Sherman.

I quickly glanced at the seating chart and then replied, "Mr. Thomas White, is it?"

"I go by Tommy," he said. "And I think Tinker Bell just flew out the window so you might want to go catch her."

Again, the class laughed. I smiled politely and waited until the room was quiet again. Tommy appeared to be gathering up his history book and backpack.

"Are you planning to go somewhere, Tommy?" I asked.

"Aren't you sending me to the principal's office?" he asked matter-of-factly.

This time I laughed. I could see that the entire class looked confused. Apparently, Mrs. Borrington did not tolerate the silly antics from a class clown. "Absolutely not! If I did, you would miss the most exciting history lesson of your life!"

"Um, for the record, history is not exciting," Tommy said. "Seriously, I have to stay?"

"Well, I hope you choose to stay," I said. "I love your imagination, Tommy. That's exactly the kind of mind I want all of you to have as we discover history together, discover the stories of the exceptional people who made us who we are today. I dress like this to help your imaginations. For as long as I can remember, my boyhood idol has been the famous American patriot Paul Revere. He was a silversmith. He took part in the Boston Tea Party. He developed a system of lanterns to warn the minutemen of a British invasion. And, of course, the event that he's most famous for is his midnight ride in April of 1775."

Tommy eased back into his chair. I could tell he wasn't convinced that history was exciting, yet. But I could see a hint of curiosity on his face.

"Imagine that it's midnight," I said. "It's very dark outside. You hear the hoot of an owl and, perhaps, see bats fly through the air under a full moon. You're on a secret mission to ride as fast as you can to warn the colonists that the British are coming! Raise your hand if you're up for the challenge!"

Several of the students raised their hands, mostly boys, including Tommy. However, I saw one girl in the back of the class who raised her hand, too, but then quickly dropped it. Hmm, I had noticed this girl earlier. She didn't laugh when the rest of the class laughed. She looked very comfortable sitting in the very last row in the corner. Her dark hair had a blue feather clipped in it. She wore jeans with a hole in one knee, but I could tell it wasn't a fashion statement. I looked at the seating chart and noticed the girl's name, Freedom. What an unusual name. Personally, I couldn't help but be a fan!

"Ah, I see we have several brave souls who are ready to ride like Paul Revere. However, in order for you to ride, you're going to need a horse." I paused. Nothing happened. This time, a little louder, I repeated every word slowly: "I said, we're going to need a horse!" I glanced at the door. I paused, again. Still nothing happened.

The students looked at me very confused.

I sighed. "We're supposed to have a special guest join us, but it appears he's running late. Excuse me while I go and see if he's lost." I walked toward the door, opened it, and glanced down the hallway. Nothing. I walked down the hall toward the front doors of the school and passed by the door to the teacher's bathroom. I paused, considering my options. I heard the toilet flush and then I heard what sounded like the clomping of horse hooves. I rolled my eyes and pushed the door open. Sure enough, there stood my horse, Liberty, admiring himself in the mirror.

"Liberty!" I shouted.

Startled, Liberty bumped into one of the bathroom stalls and knocked the door halfway off its hinges.

"You missed your cue and your entrance. I'm trying to teach a history lesson and you're an important part of that," I said.

"You really shouldn't sneak up on large mammals like that," Liberty replied. "See the damage we can cause. Not my fault. I'm the victim here. And I'm pretty sure you're a few minutes early. Besides, it's not like I wear a wristwatch or carry a smartphone," Liberty replied.

"My apologies. It would be my pleasure if you would care to join me," I said sarcastically as I held open the bathroom door for him.

"That's more like it," he said as he walked past me without looking in my direction.

Liberty stuck his head out the door and looked both ways. When he didn't see anyone, we walked toward my classroom.

"Now, remember what we talked about. We don't want to freak out the students the first day by showing them a talking horse," I said.

"Yes, yes, of course. My lips are sealed," said Liberty as he pantomimed zipping his lips with his hoof.

"Good. Now, I'm going back in. Listen for your cue."

I returned to the class and was glad to see that no one had left.

"I apologize for the delay. As I was saying, it was a midnight ride from Charlestown to Lexington when Paul Revere shouted, 'The British are coming, the British are coming!' This would not be complete or even possible without a noble and swift horse! Please welcome our special guest, Liberty!"

Liberty pushed the door open and strutted into the classroom.

The students in the front row leaned back, utterly shocked at what they were seeing.

"No way!" said Tommy. "You actually brought a horse into school? This is so cool!"

Most of the class was standing by now, watching Liberty prance around the front of the room. From the way Liberty was soaking up the attention, you'd think he was standing in the winner's circle at the Kentucky Derby.

Several students still looked flabbergasted. They watched Liberty as if he were a mythical unicorn and crowded closer to him. The girl named Freedom, however, stood five steps back from the rest of the class. Was she afraid? No, not afraid. Unsure? Yes, that's it. She was looking at the other students, unsure of whether she was welcome to join them in their new discovery.

"Don't get too close to us, Freedom," said Elizabeth, who stood at least two inches taller than the other girls in the class. "The horse might smell you and run away."

Freedom stepped back to her desk and sat down.

"Class, I assure you that Liberty is very friendly. There's no need to be alarmed. He doesn't bite and fortunately, he's potty-trained," I said, still irritated that Liberty was late.

Liberty snorted at my last comment, clearly insulted, and flicked his tail into my face. His horse hair tickled my nose and before I could stop it, I sneezed!

It happened so fast that Liberty instinctively said, "Bless you."

I froze, wondering if anyone had heard that. Liberty froze, clearly worried if I had heard that. The students froze, clearly trying to determine if they had heard that. Finally, one of the students broke the silence and slowly said, "Did your horse just say 'Bless you'?"

"My horse? T-t-talk?" I stammered, looking back and forth between the students and Liberty. "Uh, well, yes. I've taught him a couple of words, sort of like a talking parrot. Words like 'bless you.' I mean, what else do you say when someone else sneezes?" I said, trying to laugh it off.

Then, without warning, I sneezed again, "Achoo!"

This time Liberty said, "Gesundheit!"

Again, the students were wide-eyed and speechless. This was not going as planned. The *horse*, as they say, was out of the bag. So I decided to confess, sort of. I sighed, again. "The truth is Liberty is an exceptional learner. He's very bright and, of course, he loves American history. So as long as you can keep this a secret I can keep bringing Liberty to our class. Agreed?" I said, hoping it was enough.

You would have thought I had just asked if each student wanted a million dollars! A flurry of responses came rushing back at me, "Yes! Okay! I'll keep it secret! I'll do it. I'm in!"

"Well, then, it appears we're unanimous," I replied. "Wonderful." I turned to Liberty. "Is there anything you'd like to say?"

Liberty let out a big, horsey "Neighhhhhhhhhhhhhh."

The students looked at each other and then back at me. Tommy was the first to speak and said, "Not very impressive for a talking horse."

I turned to Liberty and mumbled, "Seriously, that's the best you can do?" Then I turned back to the class and laughed. "Liberty has quite the sense of humor," I said. Clearing my throat, I looked at Liberty and spread my arm toward the class and said, "Liberty, the jig is up. Your cover has been blown. Go ahead and tell the class whatever you'd like."

Liberty smiled and I could only imagine what was about to

come out of his mouth. He inhaled deeply, and then in one long breath he repeated the Preamble of the Constitution!

"*We the People* of the United States in Order to form a more perfect Union establish Justice insure domestic Tranquility provide for the common defence promote the general Welfare and secure the Blessings of Liberty to ourselves and our Posterity do ordain and establish this Constitution for the United States of America," he said, gasping for air.

Spontaneously, Liberty was showered with praises. "Awesome!" "Cool!" "Sweet!" "Unbelievable!" "No way!" "Wicked!" "Whoaaaaaa!" "Dude!"

Liberty took a bow or two.

"Show-off," I said out of the side of my mouth.

Liberty ignored me as the students came to the front of the class and surrounded him, touching and petting his mane and fur. "You're too kind," he said.

Tommy started scratching behind Liberty's neck. "Oh yes," said Liberty. "Right there, a little to the right. Yes, that's it, right behind my left ear. Ahhhhh."

"How did you say that in one breath?" Tommy asked.

"I bet you could do it if you tried," said Liberty.

I rolled my eyes and realized that my class was officially horsing around. "All right, class. Back to your seats," I said. "Show-and-tell is over. Thank you, everyone. Please be seated."

The students returned to their seats and I decided we had spent enough time on the introduction and pleasantries. "Class, I want you to put away your history books. Of course, books are wonderful, but when I'm teaching you won't need them."

"Mr. Revere," Tommy said with his hand in the air. "Not to be rude, but I'd rather hear Liberty talk."

"I knew I would love this class," Liberty said, jumping in. "You know, horses have been an important part of this country."

Oh no, I thought. Here he goes.

Liberty continued breathlessly, "You could say we're the backbone of America! We've lived among the Native Americans, we've fought in the greatest battles, we've carried all the early presidents! One of my favorite riders was George Washington! Now, he could ride. He also knew how to brush down a horse. The trick is using long strokes and starting at the top of—"

"Thank you, Liberty," I butted in. "You've been a wealth of knowledge, but I think we can save the horse-brushing lesson for another day—"

This time, Tommy butted in. "Wait, did he say he carried President George Washington? That was more than two hundred years ago."

Liberty opened his mouth and then shut it.

"I think what Liberty was trying to say is . . . well . . . he's referring to my method of teaching," I said quickly, not ready to introduce the concept of a time-traveling horse.

"That's right," Liberty said, rescuing me. "Having Rush Revere as a teacher is like going to the movies! You all like live-action movies, right?"

No surprise that the students all said yes.

I walked over and pulled down the white projector screen. "History is a mystery until it is discovered. Your job is to use your imaginations as if you're actually there. I'm going to help you. The 'movie' you are about to see will make it appear as if I've gone back in time."

Liberty winked at me.

I continued: "Your job is to try to identify where I'm at, who

I'm talking to, what event is happening, and why it is so important."

As I was speaking, Liberty walked over to the chalkboard, grabbed a piece of chalk with his teeth, and wrote, "Where? What? Who? Why?"

"Together, we're going to discover the truth about history," I said. "Are you ready?"

The students nodded. However, I could tell that Tommy was still not convinced he wanted to be here.

As Liberty walked over to dim the lights, I walked over to the digital film projector and attached a small antenna to receive signals from my smartphone. Then I gave the class one final instruction: "The movie will start in just a minute. I'm going to walk Liberty outside for a breath of fresh air. I'll return shortly."

"What about the popcorn?" Tommy asked.

"An excellent idea, Tommy," I replied. "Tomorrow, you'll have fresh buttered popcorn."

A quick flurry of cheers came from the students.

"And I'll bring the red licorice," Liberty said. "Not long ago I was watching one of my favorite movies, *Seabiscuit*. It was the final race and Seabiscuit was coming around the last bend heading for the finish line, and I, of course, was on the edge of my seat. I couldn't take my eyes off the screen so I blindly grabbed for a piece of licorice, but instead of eating it I accidentally stuffed it up my nose."

My horse, I thought, the comedian. I rolled my eyes as the class laughed. I pointed Liberty to the door at the back of the room and walked over to join him.

"When the movie is over, we'll review what you saw," I said.

Liberty and I slipped out into the hallway, and I jumped onto

Liberty's saddle. I pulled out my smartphone and tapped the camera app and switched it to video mode. As soon as Liberty jumped through the time-portal I would tap RECORD and video our adventure, which would be transmitted to the film projector back in the classroom.

It's a miracle that it works but this way the students could see and hear exactly what Liberty and I were experiencing.

"Do you have your seasickness pills?" Liberty asked.

"Already took one," I replied.

"Good, because the last time we were on the *Mayflower* you looked like green Jell-O," he said with a laugh.

"No time to spare, Liberty. Let's go!"

Liberty bounded down the hall and said, *"Rush, rush, rushing to history!"*

A vertical swirling hole of purple and gold began opening in the middle of the hallway. It grew in size as Liberty approached.

I grabbed tighter to the horn on Liberty's saddle and shouted, "Sixteen twenty, Holland, the Pilgrims!" All I could do now was hope we landed on dry ground.

Right before Liberty jumped through the time portal, I had the feeling we were being watched. I turned my head and the last thing I saw was someone's head dart back inside the classroom, someone with long dark hair and a flash of blue.

Chapter 2

The trip through the time portal was like jumping through a hoop. Instantaneously, we landed in Holland. I quickly surveyed the geography and discovered we were in a field not far from the small Dutch port of Delfshaven. Thankfully, we were alone. Wildflowers with yellow and maroon blossoms buzzed with honeybees. An apple orchard was not too far to our left.

"Oh, look, apples!" Liberty said. "My favorite!" He started trotting toward the nearest tree. "You know that apples are an excellent source of dietary fiber—and vitamin C, too?" he said. "Of course, apples also have plenty of essential minerals like potassium, calcium, magnesium—"

"Liberty, my brilliant friend," I butted in. "Your nutritional understanding of an apple is impressive, but we're here on a historical quest. Let's gather some apples and stick them in your saddlebag, quickly. We need to head over to where that ship is." I pointed to the harbor.

"Oh, all right," Liberty sighed as we began plucking apples.

I opened the saddlebag and we both dropped them in. After about twenty apples, we journeyed over to the port. I could smell the salty sea, watch the water push up and back along the beach, and hear the sound of seagulls as they soared above us. Liberty trotted toward a large gathering of people near the shore. I noticed their colorful and bright clothing.

"Pardon me," I said to a young woman wearing a long green woolen dress and a linen cap that came down over her ears. She was walking toward the shore and carrying a cat that seemed very curious about Liberty. I smiled and continued: "I'm looking for the Pilgrims, I mean, the Puritans. I understand their plan is to sail to the New World." For a split second I worried that I might have missed them. I added, "They're probably wearing dark, drab clothing. I assume the men have tall, black stovepipe hats."

The woman turned in my direction but didn't stop walking. She stared at me as if I were some strange animal at a zoo. She quickly replied, "If you're looking for the Puritans, you've found us."

These? The Puritans? I had always imagined the Pilgrims in clothing that was black, white, and gray. However, these people wore clothing that was dyed every color of the rainbow! A yellow shirt, blue breeches, green stockings, a red dress, a purple knitted stocking cap . . . I was sorely mistaken to think that I knew what the Pilgrims wore every day. It was time to get my class involved.

"Class," I said, "these are the real Pilgrims." I pointed the lens of my smartphone toward the large group that had gathered. "In the year 1620 they were known as Puritans or Saints or Separatists. Many of them separated themselves from the Church

of England and escaped to Holland, where they could practice their religion without being bullied by King James and his bishops." I pointed toward the big ship in the harbor. "I can see that several men, women, and children are boarding smaller boats to take them to that larger ship anchored in the harbor. Let's go find out the truth."

Liberty and I approached the large gathering. I called to the first man we approached and said, "Excuse me, sir, but is the ship out there the *Mayflower?*"

The man turned in my direction. He looked about thirty years old and could have passed as a movie star. He was tall with brown hair and a cleanly trimmed beard. He wore a leather hat that shaded his face from the sun, a long-sleeved light blue shirt, blue breeches, and green woolen stockings. I could see he was comforting a woman in a long woolen red dress. He had his arm around her and I could tell she was crying. I quickly said, "Oh, I'm sorry, I didn't mean to bother you."

The man looked at Liberty and then to me and said, "It's no bother. I'm not familiar with any ship called *Mayflower.* The ship out yonder is the *Speedwell.*"

That's odd, I thought. Where was the *Mayflower?*

"You look bewildered," said the kind stranger. "Can we help you? Are you looking for someone?"

"As a matter of fact, I am," I replied. "I'm looking for one of the leading members of the Puritans, a Mr. William Bradford."

Immediately, the woman stopped crying and the man stepped in front of her. He responded, "I'm William Bradford. Do you come bearing bad news?"

Surprised at my sudden discovery, I jumped off Liberty and reached out to shake his hand. "Mr. Bradford, it is an honor to meet you! I'm a big admirer and I would love to be of assistance to you." When I realized I was still shaking his hand, I let go and just smiled.

William looked back at the woman, who I assumed was his wife, and then back to me. He said, "I'm sorry, but have we met?"

"Technically, no," I replied. "But I was told I could find you here." I fudged the truth a little and continued: "You see, I'm a history teacher—an historian, of sorts, and a Pilgrim, in spirit. Your Puritan faith fascinates me and I would love to follow you to the New World."

"I see," said William. "A fellow Puritan is always welcome to join us. We are boarding the *Speedwell* now. Many of us are saying goodbye to friends and family who are staying in Holland."

"Do you mind my asking why you're leaving? This looks like a beautiful country and a wonderful place to raise a family," I said, looking around and spreading my arms as if to show William everything he was leaving behind. That's when I noticed Liberty following a man pushing a wheelbarrow loaded with large cheese wheels. I hoped the horse was behaving himself.

"Looks can be deceiving," William said. "We lived in Leiden, Holland, for twelve years, but it is not our home. Originally, we came from Scrooby, Nottinghamshire, England. But the government forced us to choose between following our faith and following the law."

"What did you do?" I asked.

"We chose to follow our faith. So we left in search of a land where we could be free to believe and worship without persecution. We found that in Holland. We even created the 'Pilgrim Press' and printed papers to help spread the word about religious freedom. But now we need a community that protects our families from evil influences. Some of our members, including our older youths, are beginning to leave the Puritan faith because of what they see and hear from our Dutch neighbors. It is for this reason we have decided to start fresh in the New World."

I nodded with understanding and said, "It appears your wife will miss this place."

William's wife quickly looked away from me. I could tell she was trying desperately not to cry, so she tearfully excused herself. William reached for her but she was now beyond his grasp.

"My wife, Dorothy, and I have decided to leave behind our three-year-old son, John. The journey is expected to be dangerous. We have wrestled in mighty prayer to know whether or not we should bring him. We believe that God has told us that John would be safer if he stayed. He will be cared for, but, as you can imagine, the decision has been particularly painful for Dorothy."

Again, I nodded, trying to show support. I knew that William and his wife were only trying to do what was best for their toddler. However, I also knew that other Pilgrims had chosen to bring their young children.

William interrupted my thoughts and said, "I apologize. I have yet to ask your name."

Before I could respond, screams turned our attention toward the shops. Women were running toward us while dodging several large cheese wheels as they rolled toward the water. I had a funny feeling I knew who was behind this. When all the cheese wheels came to a stop, I looked for Liberty. I presumed he was hiding.

I turned back to William and said, "Thank you very much for your time. I'm Rush Revere, and I look forward to visiting with you more on the *Mayflo*—" And then I remembered what

William had said. The ship the Pilgrims were boarding was not the *Mayflower*. "Is this the ship you're taking to America?" I pointed to the harbor.

"It's one of them," he said. "We purchased the *Speedwell* here in Holland. However, we need another. We have friends who are looking into hiring a ship in London. Hopefully, it'll be bigger and better than this one. We have many families and much to bring to the New World. Both ships are expected to meet in Southampton, England, before we embark for America."

I couldn't remember the fate of the *Speedwell*. Did it travel with the *Mayflower* all the way to America? Was it shipwrecked? Did it sink? I know that William Bradford sailed on the *Mayflower* to America. So he had to survive the trip back to England, but what about the other men, women, and children? I turned my thoughts again to my new Puritan friend and thoughtfully said, "I think it will be best if I meet you in England."

Confused, he asked, "Are you not traveling with us on the *Speedwell*? Do you have another ship coming for you?"

I stared at him as I searched for what to say. Finally, I replied, "Yes, well, I, um, I'm waiting for someone. And I have some supplies I still need to gather. And I . . ."

"No excuses, my friend," William said, smiling. He firmly put both hands on my shoulders and stared straight into my eyes. With great sincerity he said, "There is no need to fear. Take courage. God will bring us to the New World. Whatever adversity we face will only make us stronger." He shook my hand. "I hope whoever you're waiting for comes soon. And I hope our paths cross again. Safe travels, Rush Revere."

As he left to find his wife and board the ship with the other Pilgrims, I marveled at his courage, determination, and faith.

Before leaving for the New World in 1620, the Pilgrims prayed at the Old Church at Delfshaven, Holland.

William Bradford as a young man.

I was eager to know what happened to the *Speedwell*, curious to reach England and meet the other travelers, and eager to experience life upon the *Mayflower*. First, however, I needed to find Liberty and return to our classroom. I was very curious to know what my students had learned and a little worried to know what Liberty had been up to.

Fortunately, I didn't have to look very far to find Liberty. I heard his high-pitched whistle coming from a bright-colored shop at the corner of the street. That's when I saw his head peeking around the corner. Was he hiding? When I was close enough to speak to him I asked, "Why are you hiding behind this shop?"

"Funny you should ask," Liberty said with a grimace. "First things first: I need you to pay the shopkeeper of this store."

"You broke something," I said.

"No, I did not break something," Liberty replied. "Just because I've broken things before doesn't mean I can't be trusted to try on wooden shoes in a small Dutch shop because I want to prove to that doubtful shoemaker that horses are wonderful cloggers!"

I looked down at Liberty's hooves only to discover four bright yellow wooden shoes with red tulips painted on each of them. "Liberty, you're going to have to remove those shoes and return them immediately," I said.

"An excellent idea, theoretically," Liberty replied. "The problem is . . . I can't. They're stuck. How I got them on I have no idea. But these wooden babies are wedged on pretty tight."

I reached down and tried to pull one off. Sure enough, they stuck like superglue.

Facing page: Pilgrim woman with shawl joined by Pilgrim man with musket circa 1620.

I sighed with frustration and said, "What am I supposed to do, enter you in a horse-clogging competition? Oh, brother. Liberty, I insist that from now on you stay by my side and do exactly what I say. Your freedom to choose as you please is becoming troublesome!"

Liberty calmly replied, "You're sounding an awful lot like King James."

"Excuse me?" I asked, not sure what he meant.

He smiled and said, "Here's the thing. I'm a curious horse. I can't help it. It's just who I am. Discovering new things that interest me is what makes me happy. I love that we can travel together and discover the truth about history. But what interests you may not always be what interests me. Forcing someone else to like the things you like, or to do the things you do, is not what freedom is about, is it?"

"Of course not," I said humbly.

"From what I heard near the cheese cooler, King James didn't want the Puritans to have the freedom to choose what they believed. He just wanted them to stay with the Church of England and do exactly what he said, or else! But the Puritans believed that the Church of England practiced many things that the Bible never taught. So some Puritans called themselves 'Separatists,' because they wanted to separate themselves once and for all from the Church of England. I even heard one of the Puritan women say that the king threw an entire family into prison just because they chose to believe differently than he did."

I had a sick feeling in my stomach. I felt horrible for trying to force Liberty to do what I wanted. "I'm sorry, Liberty," I said. "You're absolutely right. Will you forgive me?"

"Of course I'll forgive you. You're not the only one who makes mistakes," he said as he lifted up a wooden shoe and waved it at me.

"All right," I said, "time for plan B." I walked into the shop, placed four gold coins on the counter, smiled at the shopkeeper, and walked back outside. "And just for the record, I hope you never feel forced to do anything. I'm glad you're a curious horse. And I'm especially glad the Pilgrims had the courage to believe and think for themselves. Otherwise, America might not be a free country." I lifted myself onto Liberty's saddle and said, "I think it's time we head back to the future!"

"Wait, you want me to run in these?" Liberty complained, staring at his shoes.

"Well, you said you could clog in them," I replied.

"Well, yes. But clogging and running are two different things."

"I won't force you," I said, smiling, "but humor me, will you? Back to modern-day America."

"This is so embarrassing," Liberty said pouting.

He willingly trotted back to the same field that we'd arrived in. His trot turned into an awkward half gallop. With a little more speed he said, "*Rush, rush, rushing from history!*"

With one jump we soared through the swirling time portal and landed back in the hallway at Manchester Middle. I knew the time portal created a sixty-second delay of any footage from my smartphone to the digital projector. We had just enough time to slip into the back of the classroom without being noticed. We watched the students as they watched Liberty and me race back through the field and jump into nothingness. The movie ended, and Liberty flipped on the classroom lights.

Tommy raised his hand and said, "Just for the record, I'm not a big fan of King James. He sounds like a real party pooper. He probably got too many wedgies when he was a kid."

"As you can imagine, these Pilgrims weren't big fans of the king, either," I replied.

"They should've just done what the king told them to do," Elizabeth blurted out.

Surprised, I turned to Elizabeth and asked, "Do you do everything someone tells you to do?"

Elizabeth rolled her eyes and looked at the girl next to her. That girl, who I assume was one of Elizabeth's groupies, raised her hand and said, "What Elizabeth is trying to say is that no one tells her what to do."

"Ahh," I said. "Well, then it sounds like you would've made a great King James."

"You mean Queen James," Elizabeth said, suddenly realizing she had just called herself by a boy's name.

Several students tried to cover up their laughs but Tommy couldn't resist and said, "Hey, James. What's up?" He put his hand in the air as if to give Elizabeth a high five.

She ignored him.

"In all seriousness," Tommy said, "I liked that William Bradford dude. He was cool. Too bad he and his wife didn't bring their little guy with them."

"Let me ask everyone the same question. If you were William Bradford, would you have taken your three-year-old son on a death-defying voyage across a tempestuous sea?"

I heard several halfhearted responses. "Probably." "Maybe." "I think so." "I guess."

I had almost forgotten about Freedom until she raised her

hand like the tallest mast on the *Mayflower*. "Freedom, you have an opinion?"

Freedom's dark eyes reminded me of that same determined stare that William Bradford gave me right before he boarded the *Speedwell*. Freedom spoke from somewhere deep within and said, "I could tell they loved their son, more than anything. They only wanted what was best for him. It took courage for the Pilgrims to leave their homes and travel into the unknown. But it takes more courage to travel into the unknown and leave someone you love behind."

"Well said, Freedom," I replied. "And who knows, maybe they thought they could come back for him someday. Or maybe someone else had planned to bring him to America when he was older. I don't know. What we do know is that more than anything, the Pilgrims like William and Dorothy Bradford were real people ready to give their lives for their freedom, no matter the cost, no matter the pain, no matter the sacrifice."

Suddenly, something yellow shot from the back of the room and would have struck me in the head if I hadn't dodged it at the last second before impact. It hit the chalkboard behind me and splintered into several pieces.

From the back of the classroom, Liberty's eyes were as wide as cannonballs. With a surprised smile he said, "By golly, those wooden shoes do come off! I was beginning to wonder. I think a larger size would've fit better. Of course, now it's going to be rather difficult to clog in only three shoes. Anyway, the trick to getting them off is to leverage this hoof like this and wedge the other by pushing down like that and . . ." Again, the second shoe shot off like a rock from a slingshot, but this time it whizzed to the left and crashed through an outside window.

"Oops," Liberty said.

I rolled my eyes, but before I could say anything else the door to the classroom opened. Principal Sherman walked in, looking alarmed, and asked, "Did I just hear the sound of breaking glass?" His eyes locked on the broken window. "How did this happen?" He turned to the class and then to me and asked, "Is anyone hurt? How did the window break?"

Curious, the entire class turned around to look at Liberty, and I wondered why Principal Sherman wasn't equally alarmed at the fact that there was an actual horse standing at the back of the classroom. However, upon further inspection, Liberty was gone.

"Well, is anyone going to answer me?" Principal Sherman asked again. "Mr. Revere, do you have an explanation?"

"An explanation?" I stalled. "Well, yes, of course." I realized that Principal Sherman would eventually find a yellow wooden shoe outside the classroom window so I began: "We were discussing the Pilgrims and how they left England to escape religious persecution and settled in Holland along their journey to the New World. I brought a wooden Dutch shoe from my trip to the Netherlands as a bit of show-and-tell and—"

Principal Sherman interrupted me and said pointing, "You mean like the one that's broken and splintered on the floor here?"

I had forgotten about that one. "Yes, and apparently, wooden shoes are not very sturdy."

Principal Sherman walked over to the window and saw the second wooden shoe lying on the grass near a big oak tree. "And yet that one looks just fine," he said.

I joined him by the window and said, "Um, wood is stronger than glass?"

He was not amused. He continued his classroom interrogation: "I've still not heard a reasonable explanation for why the window is broken."

"Yes, I was getting to that," I said, wondering if this would be my last day teaching at Manchester Middle School. "Let me start by saying this has been an excellent class and—"

Before I could finish whatever it was I was going to say, Tommy jumped up from his seat and shouted, "I did it!"

I was not expecting that.

Principal Sherman took a deep breath and didn't look a bit surprised.

I could not let Tommy take the fall for Liberty's antics. "I can assure you that it was somewhat of a bizarre accident," I said.

"Yes, I'm very well acquainted with Tommy's 'accidents.' But not everyone loves a class clown. Tommy, you'll report to my office as soon as class is over," said Principal Sherman, who nearly growled when he finished.

"If you'll permit me, Principal, I have an appropriate consequence for Tommy's outburst," I said.

"Continue," the principal said while straightening his tie.

"We both know how much Tommy lo-o-o-o-oves history," I said. "I think the appropriate punishment is to keep him after for detention in my class. I'm happy to give him an extra history lesson that he's bound to never forget."

I could see that Principal Sherman was pondering the idea and examining Tommy's reaction. Tommy didn't disappoint. His face showed pure misery. The principal smiled and said, "I like that! In addition, Tommy will write on the chalkboard, 'I will not throw wooden shoes through glass windows' one hundred times."

"I like your style, Principal Sherman," I said.

"And I like yours, Mr. Revere, especially that tricornered hat. I need to get one of those," he said. "I'll have the custodian clean up and repair the window immediately." With that he turned his huge shoulders and exited the classroom.

Relieved, I let out a long breath.

"What happened to Liberty? How did he get out of the room so fast?" Tommy asked. I could hear several other students ask similar questions.

Thankfully, I was saved by the bell before I had to answer their questions. Class was over. As the students grabbed their backpacks, I said, "Tomorrow, we'll continue the journey with the Pilgrims. Thank you, everyone. Class dismissed."

As the students began filing out of the room, I noticed that Tommy stayed behind for his detention and extra history lesson.

I noticed that Freedom stayed as well. I was pretty sure that it was her head I saw dart back into the classroom just as Liberty and I had jumped through the time portal.

If I didn't know any better I'd think Freedom was on to me.

Chapter 3

*F*reedom crossed her arms and leaned back in her chair. Tommy looked back at Freedom and then back to me, shrugging his shoulders. Freedom stared at me like I might disappear if she looked anywhere else. I finally asked, "Freedom, is there something I can do for you?"

She was twisting her hair between her fingers. I could tell she was pondering whether she wanted to say something or not. She looked across the room at Tommy and then back at me. She was a pretty girl with very tan skin. She flipped back the blue feather in her hair and then pushed the rest of her long black hair behind her shoulders. Finally, she spoke and said, "He never left."

"Excuse me?" I asked. "I'm not sure I understand what you're referring to." Actually, I knew exactly what she was referring to, but I decided to play dumb.

"Liberty, he's still in the room," she calmly said. "I can

smell him. Horses have a strong scent. And if you look closely, you can see his image outlined against the back wall." Still sitting at her chair, she turned around and traced Liberty's outline with her finger.

"I don't see anything," Tommy said as he strained to see what Freedom was pointing at.

It was apparent that Freedom had a gift. She acted as sure as if she were pointing at the sun. Questions raced through my head. Could I trust these students about the time-travel abilities that Liberty and I enjoyed? Would they be able to keep the secrets about our historical missions? I decided to take a chance and said, "As I mentioned earlier, Liberty is an extraordinary horse. In addition to his language skills, he has the ability to disappear."

"Not disappear," said Freedom. "He's blending into his surroundings like a chameleon."

Suddenly, Liberty reappeared right where Freedom had pointed, gasping for air. "I couldn't . . . hold my breath . . . a second longer," said Liberty, still trying to catch his breath.

"What the . . . !" Tommy exclaimed. He looked at Freedom, then to me, then back at Liberty. "Did he just appear out of thin air? That's awesome! I mean, that's the coolest trick ever! How do you do that?"

Explaining the impossible is never easy, but I tried my best and said, "Soon after Liberty and I met we discovered that when Liberty holds his breath he can turn invisible. Well, he's invisible to most people," I said, glancing at Freedom. "It's sort of like when you hold your breath and your face begins to turn red or even purple. When you let out the air, the color in your face returns to normal. It's the same principle with Liberty."

"Except he turns invisible," Tommy said. "Coolest. Thing. Ever."

"Frankly, I'm surprised that Freedom can see through the disguise," I said. "I've seen Liberty vanish at least a hundred times and I'm still not always sure if he's in the same room."

Freedom smiled and replied, "I've had lots of practice tracking animals with my grandfather."

Tommy walked over and touched Liberty on the back just to make sure he was real. "That is so cool how you can change like that," Tommy said.

Liberty smiled and said, "I think we need a name, you know, since we all know the secret. We could be the Four Musketeers! Or the Fantastic Four! Or the Four Amigos! Or—"

Tommy started laughing and said, "Your horse cracks me up!"

"Don't encourage him," I pleaded.

"I like him, too," said Freedom. "But he is more than a horse. He must be a spirit animal. There is an Indian legend about animals that can talk to humans."

I pondered the idea and replied, "I don't know Liberty's whole story. Even Liberty doesn't know what happened exactly. Liberty, tell them what you remember the day you traveled to modern-day America."

Liberty cleared his throat and slowly began: "It was a dark and stormy night. . . ."

"Liberty!"

"Seriously, it was! I don't remember the year but I do remember that in the evening we used only candles and lanterns. Oh, and I remember George Washington. Oh, and Paul Revere. His story is one of my favorites because who doesn't love the fact that he was racing a horse to warn the Minutemen that the British were coming. I mean, if you ask me, the horse is the real hero."

I jumped in and said, "I've concluded that Liberty is originally from the revolutionary time period and lived during the Revolutionary War. His memory is spotty, but he has several strong memories during the 1770s. The Boston Tea Party, the ride of Paul Revere, the Battle of Bunker Hill, the public reading of the Declaration of Independence . . ."

"And I specifically remember hearing that in 1775 Alexander Cummings invented the flushing toilet!" exclaimed Liberty.

"I've never heard you mention that," I said, surprised.

"It just popped into my head," Liberty replied.

"But that doesn't explain how Liberty ended up in modern-day America," said Tommy.

"Or the fact that he can talk and turn practically invisible," Freedom added.

"Yes, well, let me try to explain," I said. "Liberty remembers a lightning storm—"

Liberty butted in: "I'm not a big fan of lightning. Just the thought of it gives me the willies."

I continued: "It appears that lightning may have struck Liberty and created a supernatural phenomenon or a time portal that thrust him forward in time to our day. The electrical properties that charged through his body and the vortex that sent him to the future changed him physically and mentally. He can not only talk and disappear, but he's also . . ." I paused, trying to formulate the right words.

Freedom finished my sentence and said, "A time machine."

"What?" Tommy said, confused. "Did I miss something? Did you just say 'time machine'?"

"He's more like a time portal," I said, to clarify. "He has the ability to momentarily open a time door to anywhere in history. Well, more specifically, anything that touches American history."

Tommy started laughing. "Okay, this is a joke. I'm onto you. This is some reality TV show called 'The Biggest Bozo Who Believes Anything,' right? Where are the cameras?" Tommy started looking around the room. He then looked at Freedom and back at me; both of us were dead serious.

"You believe this guy?" Tommy asked Freedom, sticking his thumb out at me.

Freedom replied, "You've just seen and heard a talking horse who turned invisible, but you won't believe he can travel through time?"

"Hey, I might be crazy, but I'm not that crazy, okay?" Tommy said. He got up from his desk and started pacing the floor. He took off his baseball cap and combed his fingers through his blond hair. He sighed, "I have to think about this for a minute."

"We probably shouldn't show them the other thing I can do, should we? I mean, he seems a little freaked out right now," Liberty said.

"No," I said, firmly. I took a deep breath. "I need to finish our story. I believe the lightning created the time portal that brought Liberty to the modern day."

Tommy put his baseball cap back on and said, "Okay, okay. Maybe it is possible. I mean, I don't think the lightning hit him directly. Technically, a direct hit would have killed him. But I guess there's a possibility that several bolts could have simultaneously hit the ground around him, creating an electrostatic prism, and maybe the positive and negative charge carriers combined with the acoustic shock waves created some kind of time hole that sent Liberty to the future."

Freedom and I were stunned by Tommy's explanation.

"Aren't you a football player?" Freedom said. "You're never this smart in our other classes."

"Yeah, well, I really wouldn't fit in with the other guys on the team if I admitted that I'm a science geek," Tommy replied.

I patted Tommy on the shoulder and said, "Exceptional thinking, Tommy. Now then, where was I, oh yes, when Liberty arrived in our time he appeared at the intersection of Washington Boulevard and Lincoln Avenue in front of that iced-tea factory. It was late at night and I was leaving the factory dressed as Paul Revere."

"Wait, you were dressed like Paul Revere? Like you are now?" asked Tommy.

"Yes, that's right," I said. "I'd been hired as part of a promotional campaign. My Paul Revere self was printed on banners, billboards, buses, even on the side of bottles. It was rather embarrassing but it paid good money. Anyway, as I was saying, I was leaving the factory dressed as Paul Revere when I had the strangest feeling I was being followed."

Liberty was nearly trotting in place and excitedly said, "Oh, oh, oh, can I tell this part? I was so happy to see someone I recognized. Well, I mean, I'd never met Rush Revere before but I recognized his clothing. It was the only thing that felt like home. I first saw him on a billboard and then on the side of a bus. And when I saw him walking out of the iced-tea factory I was like, 'Ahhhhhhhh! That's him!' But there were all these traffic lights and cars and horns and they sort of freaked me out because I'd never seen or heard any of these things before, so I was like, 'Ahhhhhhhh!' I ran across the street, weaved my way through traffic, and nearly stopped when I smelled the heavenly scent coming from the peanut vendor, and I was like, 'Ahhhhhhhh!' It smelled so good! But I couldn't stop because I didn't want to lose sight of Rush Revere. I knew he could help me so I started following him."

"That's right," I said. "And after weaving my way through town for a couple of miles I realized that the strange horse, no offense, was not giving up. Of course, I was very curious why a horse without a rider would be following me. I decided to simply stop walking and wait for him to catch up."

"I'm glad you did, but if I were you there's no way I would've stopped. I mean you might be a mugger or a zombie or even worse, a vacuum cleaner salesman!" Liberty said.

I continued: "Anyway, I had to pinch myself several times when Liberty starting talking. And when we discovered he had the ability to open a time portal I was reluctant to jump through. Nevertheless, I did and it was the beginning of our adventures through history."

Tommy turned to Freedom and said, "You realize we can't tell anyone about this. Seriously, Mr. Revere would get fired and, even worse, I'd probably get invited to join the Chess Club."

"What's so bad about the Chess Club?" Freedom asked defensively.

"Sorry I brought it up. It's just that at a different school I was in a chess club. One word, *boring*! No competition. I pretty much wasted everybody. And then all these chess nerds followed me around like I was their king. No thank you."

"There's no reason why anyone else needs to know about our secret of time travel," I said. I turned to Freedom and asked, "I'm fairly certain you saw Liberty and me jump through the time portal earlier today, correct?"

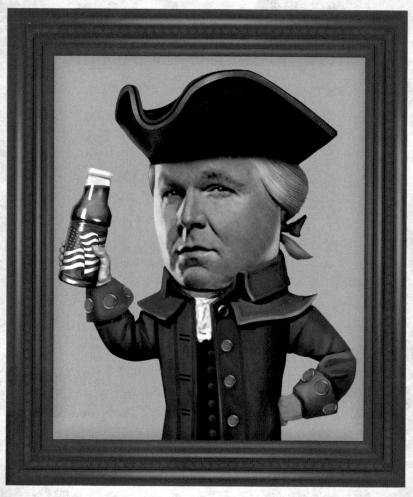

Two if by Tea®

Freedom nodded and said, "Yes, I did. At first I wasn't sure what I saw. As I said, I thought Liberty must have been a spirit animal. Maybe you were a great shaman. I did not know. But I'm glad to know the truth."

"So, wait a minute," Tommy said, "are you saying that when we saw you in the movie, you were actually time-traveling, literally?"

"I know it's hard to believe," I said. "But as the saying goes, 'seeing is believing.' Liberty, I think it's time for another history lesson. Tommy, are you ready to experience firsthand some American history?"

Tommy looked at Freedom, then to Liberty, who nodded wildly, and then back to me. He finally said, "You mean, now? We can do that? I mean, of course I want to go. My football coach won't be happy that I skipped practice, but," Tommy said laughing, "I'll just blame it on the new substitute history teacher. Oh, and I need to be home for dinner or my mom won't be happy, either."

"No problem," I said, "and, Freedom, how about you?"

Freedom glanced at the clock on the wall and looked disappointed. "My grandfather will be here to pick me up any minute," she said. "Can I go another time?"

"Absolutely," I said.

"Thanks," Freedom replied. "I better go. I'm sure my grandfather is waiting." She grabbed her backpack and started for the door. She looked over her shoulder and said, "Bye, Mr. Revere; bye, Tommy; bye, Liberty."

Freedom stared intently at Liberty one last time. She winked and exited the classroom.

"Did you just hear that?" Liberty asked.

"Hear what?" Tommy questioned.

"I heard Freedom's voice echo in my head. She said, *Don't have too much fun without me*, right before she left the classroom," said Liberty.

Fascinating, I thought.

"Maybe you just imagined it," said Tommy.

"Help me rearrange these desks so Liberty has some running room," I said.

We quickly pushed the desks to the sides of the room. I climbed up onto Liberty's saddle and invited Tommy to join me.

"Where are we going?" Tommy asked, sounding a bit unsure.

"The *Mayflower*, of course," I said.

"Uh, I've never been on a ship before," Tommy said sheepishly.

"Good to know," I said. "If you feel yourself getting nauseous I have medicine for motion sickness. But I don't want to give it to you unless you really need it."

Tommy said, "Let's hope I don't need it."

"Before I have you get on Liberty, I want you to watch what's going to happen. Liberty will open a literal time portal right here in this classroom. He and I will jump through first. We'll find you some seventeenth-century clothing and then return for you."

"What? You don't think people in 1620 are wearing blue jeans, sneakers, and a T-shirt that says 'Manchester Football'?" Tommy winked.

I smiled back and said, "I happen to know that American football wasn't started until 1879, so the answer would be no."

"We'll be back in a flash!" Liberty said.

Tommy looked doubtful. "So, I should just sit down and watch this? What exactly is going to happen? Is lightning involved? I mean, that's how it happened the first time, right?"

"It's a bit hard to explain," I said. "That's why I want you to sit this one out and just watch."

"Can we get you anything while we're gone? Something to snack on. A beverage, perhaps?" Liberty asked.

Tommy plopped down at a random desk along the side of the room, grabbed his backpack, and pulled out a Snickers bar. "I'm good. I'll just sit here and play WordSlammaJamma on my phone. Just before class I got my highest score, 126 points with the word *quillback*."

"What's a quillback? Some kind of porcupine?" Liberty asked.

"No, it's a fish. A carpsucker, actually. Pretty common in lakes on the east coast. They're easy to spot because one ray of their dorsal fin is longer than . . . oh, sorry, sometimes my inner nerd comes out," Tommy said, apologetically. He took a bite of his candy bar. "So, how long is this trip of yours going to take?"

"You'd be surprised what can happen with a time-traveling horse," I said, winking. "Let's go, Liberty."

As Liberty started galloping he said, *"Rush, rush, rushing to history!"*

The time portal started to open. Tommy watched as a circular pattern of gold and purple swirled in the center of the classroom and quickly expanded until it was the size of a large satellite dish. Liberty jumped through the center and disappeared. A second later the portal closed. Tommy was still chewing his first bite of Snickers when the time portal reopened and Liberty jumped back into the classroom.

"Cool!" Tommy said as he jumped out of his seat. "That was whacked-out! The portal thingy! I saw it! There were these swirling colors and then you jumped through and vanished. That was crazy! Seriously, I saw it but I still don't believe it. Wait, why are you back so soon? Did you forget something?" Tommy asked, confused.

"We're finished. We have your clothes," I said, pulling my traveling bag over my shoulder and tossing it on the floor near the desk Tommy was sitting at.

"And we brought you back a freshly baked carp pie," said Liberty.

"You got me a what?" Tommy asked.

"A carp pie," Liberty clarified. "You know, like a meat pie, but with fish. You seemed so excited about the word *quillback* that I thought you would enjoy eating it. It looks delicious, I mean, if you're into that sort of thing. Personally, I'm a vegetarian, but the cook seasoned it with pepper and salt and nutmeg and then baked it with raisins, lemon juice, and slices of orange peels with just a sprinkle of vinegar, and voilà!"

I opened the lid of the serving tray to show Tommy the seventeenth-century dish. He swallowed his bite of candy bar and looked at the fish like it was an alien artifact from Mars.

"How is this possible? You weren't gone for more than five seconds," Tommy managed to say.

"Well, it actually took us closer to an hour," I said. "We had to visit two different clothiers to find all the items I was looking for. I hope it all fits. And then Liberty was absolutely set on getting you this carp pie. I must admit, it was very thoughtful of him."

I covered the fish with the lid and Tommy took the tray, not really knowing what to do with it.

I said, "When it was time to come back to the modern day, Liberty returned to the present at the same time we'd left, give or take a few seconds."

"I told you we'd be back in a flash," Liberty said, smiling.

"You can do that?" Tommy asked. "I mean, I guess you can because you did. Sorry, still trying to wrap my head around the fact that time travel is even possible."

"Don't think about it too much," I said. "Why don't you take the bag, slip down to the bathroom, and change. When you get back, we'll all jump through the time portal and begin our voyage on the *Mayflower*."

"Um, okay, sure. Sounds good to me," Tommy said. "Oh, and thanks for the fish. Not much time to eat it now. Maybe I can just leave it in the classroom and then when we return back to the present in a 'few seconds' it should still be warm, right?"

"You catch on fast," I said.

Tommy set the tray on the teacher's desk, grabbed the bag of clothes, and left the room. He returned a few minutes later looking like a seventeenth-century Pilgrim boy. He wore a short-sleeved, off-white linen shirt with a collar. Over that he wore a blue doublet that buttoned down in the front. In addition, he wore green baggy breeches, yellow stockings, leather shoes, and instead of his red baseball cap he wore a brown wide-brimmed hat. Tommy handed me the bag with his modern-day clothes, pointed to what he was now wearing, and said, "I assume you intended me to wear these clothes, right? There was a dress in the bag, too, but it really wasn't my style."

I chuckled. "I forgot about that. Yes, I purchased a dress for Freedom. I thought she might need it the next time we time-jump." I slipped the bag into a bottom drawer in the teacher's desk.

Tommy lifted his heel out of his shoe and put it back again. "For the record, these shoes need some padded insoles. And these pants, what are they called again?"

"Breeches," I said.

"Yeah, these breeches are really itchy."

"Well, you look great!" I said from on top of Liberty's saddle. "Now jump up behind me."

Tommy seemed unsure of what to do and said, "I've never been on a horse before."

"No worries," I said, "we'll make this easy. Liberty, walk over to the teacher's desk so Tommy can climb on from there."

When Tommy was sitting behind me I said, "Hold on to the saddle. Liberty is a smooth jumper and he's getting better at where he lands, but just in case. . . ."

"For the record," Liberty defended, "I've been one hundred percent accurate since we accidentally landed in Boston Harbor."

"Let's not forget the Civil War battlefield," I reminded him.

"Well, it's hard to forget when you keep bringing it up. Back then I was a novice, but I think I've come a long way, not to mention that I did save you from that cannonball."

"What cannonball?" Tommy asked, curiously.

"A story for another time," I said. "Liberty, we need to land undetected on the *Mayflower*."

"Got it!" said Liberty as he galloped forward. "*Rush, rush, rushing to history!*"

The time portal opened just as it did moments earlier. As clearly as possible, I pronounced each word, "September sixth, 1620, Plymouth, England, the launching of the *Mayflower*." I had found that giving the exact date, location, and name of the historical event helped Liberty get us to where we needed to be.

The sensation of jumping through time was always the same. A rush of air sent goose bumps all over my body, the hair on my arms stood on end, and for a split second it felt like it does when

you're swinging backward on a swing set. Yes, backward, probably because we were heading backward in time. The sensation happened only when we were airborne and passing through the portal. Once we landed, the feeling was gone.

Two seconds later, we landed on what looked like a cobblestone street behind some large crates and barrels. As we peered out from behind the cargo we immediately saw a large sailing vessel about a hundred feet in length and twenty-five feet wide that was moored alongside a stone wharf. Three tall masts with square-rigged sails stood like the queen's guards at Buckingham Palace as men, women, and children carrying few possessions walked down a dozen or so stone steps and then crossed over a wooden gangplank to board the ship.

"That's it!" I exclaimed. "That's the legendary *Mayflower* with the original Pilgrims as they board to sail to the New World! This is truly an exceptional moment for America. This little ship with a hundred and two passengers is going to cross the wide Atlantic Ocean, more than three thousand miles, with no guarantee that they're going to make it. Imagine how nervous or scared you might feel."

"Thank you, Captain Positive, for the pep talk," said Liberty.

"Let's try and board with the Pilgrims," I said. "Liberty, I doubt they'll let a horse on the ship so you'll need to follow closely behind and stay under cover."

"Ten-four. Going into stealth mode in three, two, one," Liberty said as he took a giant breath and disappeared.

"How will we get on if they have a passenger list?" asked Tommy as we walked toward the ship. "What if they don't have any more room for two more passengers?"

"I happen to know that many of the Pilgrims had second thoughts about traveling to the New World and decided to stay in England," I said.

"You mean they were nervous or scared about going?" Tommy asked.

I nodded, then continued. "Yes, and I imagine others were persuaded not to go by family or friends. Or perhaps the trip from Holland to England made them realize that a longer voyage to the New World would be more than they could handle. Right up before the *Mayflower* left for the New World there were many passengers who changed their minds and 'jumped ship,' as they say."

"Well, then, they might be happy to see us," Tommy said.

As we reached the gangplank William Bradford recognized me and said, "Rush Revere! It does my heart good to see you again. And is this the person you were waiting for in Holland?" He smiled affectionately while straightening Tommy's brown leather hat.

"Yes, this is Tommy," I said as I put my arm around Tommy's shoulder. "His parents are gone so I'll be caring for him on this voyage."

"It's a pleasure to meet you, Tommy," Bradford said as he reached out his hand to Tommy, who shook it. William turned back to me and said, "Let's talk some more after the ship sets sail. The captain is very eager to leave. He says the winds are perfect. We're just waiting for one more family and . . . oh, here they come. Wonderful. We should be leaving in a minute or two."

"We'll wait for you on deck. It'll be an honor to talk some more with you," I said with great enthusiasm.

Robert W. Weir's rendering of Pilgrims embarking from Delfshaven, Holland, on July 22, 1620. William Brewster (holding the Bible), William Bradford, Myles Standish, and their families. This painting is on display in the U.S. Capitol Building Rotunda.

Pilgrims and "Strangers" boarding small boats heading toward the *Mayflower* in Plymouth, England, 1620.

Boatloads of people waving farewell to the *Mayflower* as she leaves Plymouth for America, September 6, 1620. Original Artwork: after Gustave Alaux.

We continued past William and crossed the gangplank to board the *Mayflower*. As I stepped onto the upper deck a chill went through my body. The kind of sensation you get when you walk into the front gates of Disneyland. Or the feeling you have when you wake up knowing that it's Christmas morning!

"Unbelievable," said Tommy. "I just checked my phone and it says I have service. Not sure how that's possible but I think I'll send Freedom a text from the *Mayflower*. Let's walk over closer to the bow where we can take a picture without anyone watching. Plus if Liberty is behind us he'll want a place to get another breath of air."

"Good idea," I said.

Seagulls flew overhead, their calls competing with about a hundred or so passengers who were crowded near the aft and starboard quarter of the ship. I assumed they were calling to family and friends who were standing near the steps of the wharf. The sailors were calling back and forth to each other as large sails plumed from the square rigging. It was time to sail. The gangplank had disappeared and the ship was no longer anchored to the wharf. We were drifting out to sea!

As the ship rocked leeward for the first time, Tommy stumbled to the ship's railing as if he had just entered an ice-skating rink without ever having ice-skated.

"I'm good," he said. "I guess I don't have my sea legs yet. I'll get the hang of it." He let go of the railing and balanced himself with his hands out to his sides as if he were surfing. "This is so awesome."

I smiled at Tommy as he continued to "surf" but I was also curious to know where Liberty was. I called, "Liberty?" There was no sight of him and no answer. I looked over the ship's railing to see if I could spot him somewhere on the wharf. I didn't see him. Tommy saw the concern in my eyes. Oh boy, I thought. It's one thing to lose a cat or dog. But I wasn't sure how to start searching for a lost magical horse!

Chapter 9

"*The captain don't* like passengers snoopin' around his ship!" someone yelled behind us.

We spun around and saw a sailor who wore an off-white long-sleeved shirt, a dingy orange vest, and a dark blue knit cap. He had a black scraggly beard and a thin scar along the side of his cheek. He climbed down off the forecastle and landed sure-footed on the upper deck of the *Mayflower*.

"We're just, um, exploring the ship. Is there a problem?" I asked in my most convincing British accent.

The sailor looked at us as if he was still digesting what he saw. In a gruff voice he said, "Yeah, you're the problem. You're another Puritan, aren't you."

It didn't sound like a question, nor did it sound friendly, but I responded anyway. "We're traveling with the Puritans as they travel to the New World, if that's what you're asking."

As the sailor walked closer I had a déjà vu moment. He

looked very familiar. Had we met before? Perhaps he looked like someone from the future. I couldn't put my finger on it.

"I'm sick and tired of all you Puritans," the sailor said. "I'm sick of your praying and your holier-than-thou attitude. You should've all stayed in Plymouth with the others. Better yet, I wish the *Speedwell* would've sunk and taken the lot of you with her. It was bad enough having some of you on the *Mayflower*. Now I'm stuck with all of you."

I must admit I was surprised by this sailor's hatefulness against the Puritans.

The sailor gave a wicked smile and said, "I guess there's one good reason to have you on board."

"That's the spirit," I said.

Tommy nudged me and whispered, "I don't think this is going to be a compliment."

The sailor continued: "We'll have plenty of food for the sharks!" He laughed.

Suddenly, I remembered where I'd seen him. Of course—he was the sailor that I encountered the first time I had time-traveled to the *Mayflower*. How could I forget the person who almost threw me overboard? Obviously, he wouldn't remember that first meeting, because for him that part of history hadn't happened yet.

Just then Liberty appeared directly in front of the sailor, deliberately snorted, took another deep breath, and then disappeared.

I think I was just as surprised as the sailor. On second thought, maybe not. The sailor had slimy horse snot oozing down his face.

"What the . . . where did . . . that was a . . . ," the sailor muttered as he tried to wipe away the snot.

"Rush Revere!" a voice called from the front of the ship.

The sailor quickly went about his business as if he had not been talking with us. I turned around to see who had called my name. I was thrilled to see my Pilgrim hero William Bradford walking toward me with his wife, Dorothy.

"Rush, you joined us in the nick of time," said William.

"Yes, well, better late than never," I said, laughing.

We all had to catch our balance as the bow of the ship plowed over a wave. A light spray of water splashed over the ship's railing. The large sails of the *Mayflower* no longer rippled like they did closer to the coast. Out in the open ocean they billowed like parachutes, pushing the boat westward.

William said, "You get used to that after a while. Have you had time to tour the ship?"

"No, not really," I said. "I was just talking with Tommy. He's a bit lonely without his horse. But there really isn't any room for a horse on the *Mayflower,* is there?" I asked, hoping I'd get the answer I was looking for.

"Unfortunately, no," said William. "The only place I can think of where a horse might fit and stay protected from the wind and waves is the capstan room."

Bingo.

"What's a capstan?" asked Tommy.

"And where's the capstan room?" I asked, hoping Liberty was paying attention.

"The room is located on this deck but it's at the aft of the ship. The capstan is kind of a pulley," said William. "It's used to move heavy cargo between decks."

"Thank you," I said. "Very interesting. Well, I'm hopeful we can find and train another horse when we get to the New World."

Mayflower II in calm seas.

"How many decks are there on the *Mayflower?*" asked Tommy. "I mean, where do people sleep?"

"Good question," said William. He pointed toward the top aft end of the ship, "That up there is the quarterdeck. That's where you'll find the captain's cabin. The deck we're standing on is the upper deck. The galley or ship's kitchen is to the bow."

I knew Liberty wasn't around or he would have asked for a personal tour of the kitchen and then he would have volunteered to be the *Mayflower's* official taste tester!

"Below this deck is the tween deck. That's where most of the passengers are living and sleeping. We also have a small pen for our smaller livestock, including chickens. And below the tween deck is the cargo hold where we store our flour, barrels of water, and other general supplies."

"William," I asked, "tell me, how are things for you? How can I help with your voyage?"

"Our numbers are dwindling. There used to be nearly one hundred and fifty Puritans traveling to the New World. But the trip has been hard on many of our people. After several attempts of trying to sail two ships to America we decided that the *Speedwell* was not seaworthy. It leaked like a sieve. Three times the crew tried to patch her up, without success. The first attempt was at Southampton after a very wet and worrisome journey from Holland. But a leaky ship will not keep us from the freedom we desperately want. We will make it to our new home!"

That's when William gave me the most reassuring smile. It's no wonder the Pilgrims were ready to follow him to the New World. He was inspiring to listen to. I was ready to follow him, too.

"You said that there used to be nearly one hundred and fifty Puritans," I said. "How many are there now?"

"The passengers of the *Mayflower* include about fifty Puritans. The crew refers to us as Saints. The other half are Adventurers, also known as Strangers."

Tommy whispered in my ear, "Sounds like two football teams playing on *Monday Night Football*, the Saints versus the Strangers."

I smiled as William continued: "We had to include others if we stand a chance of starting a new settlement in the New World. It's not ideal but it's a step closer in getting us to our new home."

"I really like your ship," said Tommy. "And I happen to know you'll make it to the New World."

"Really?" William said, smiling. "You say that without a shadow of a doubt in your voice. I wish more of our members had your same positive attitude and conviction."

A gust of wind came up and William quickly grabbed for his hat. He looked up at the sails and said, "I believe that heaven is helping us. We should give thanks for such a prosperous wind. Come, let us find Elder Brewster."

As we followed William, the boat rose and fell with greater force. The winds were getting stronger and the swells were getting bigger. We were far out to sea now. Dark clouds pushed across the Atlantic Ocean. More frequently, water splashed up and over the ship's railing. Imagine what it would be like in the evening when it was pitch black outside. Waves crashing, winds howling, thunder cracking, and the ship rocking fiercely against the waves. I imagined a monstrous wave that rocked the ship so hard that it capsized. The thought was terrifying and I quickly pushed it from my mind. It was easy for me to do because

I knew that the *Mayflower* made it to the New World. But none of the Pilgrims knew that. And yet, William Bradford spoke as if he did know. His faith allowed him to stay optimistic despite the raging storm.

We arrived at the hatch door that led down to the between decks. Other passengers were lined up and climbing down the ladder. When we were close enough to climb down, the smell caught my attention immediately. Tommy whispered, "Whoa, this is ten times worse than our locker room at school. It smells like a boatload of stinky socks down there."

As quietly as possible I responded, "There should be about a hundred people down there, with no windows and not a lot of room."

"That's like the time we had our family reunion at my house and like a hundred of my relatives crammed into my living room for a few hours. It was so crowded and most of my cousins are really annoying."

"That was just for a few hours," I said. "Now try it for a few weeks or months and instead of your relatives you have to hang with a bunch of people from your church and the other half is a bunch of people you've never met."

Tommy's eyes were wide with concern. "Seriously? All in the same room? Oh, that would get old really fast. I mean, I think an hour would be too long with some people. And the smell down there must be a lot stronger. I don't know how they did it."

Tommy followed William and I followed Tommy.

When I stepped from the bottom rung of the ladder to the tween deck I had to bend my knees and lean forward to enter the room. Tommy was standing up straight but it looked like his head touched the wood ceiling. Hunched over, we tried to follow William through a maze of people. The only light that came into the room was from the open hatch. It was dim but there was enough light to see that every family had a small living space. Some families had built wooden dividers that served as walls and provided them with a little privacy. We heard voices all around us; many of them were children saying things like:

"How long do we have to stay down here?"

"The sea is making me sick again."

"I have to go potty."

"Can I go find the puppy?"

I thought that last comment was odd, but with all the voices it was hard to be sure what I heard. Occasionally, water dripped through the upper deck and onto my head and neck. Tommy tapped me on the shoulder and whispered, "This place is creepy. And I think someone or something is following me."

"Not to worry," I whispered back. "We won't stay long."

Suddenly, a little boy, probably five or six years old, jumped out of the darkness and into our path. He looked up at Tommy and said, "Pardon me, but have you seen the puppy?"

Tommy crouched down until he was eye to eye with the little boy and said, "Sorry, little dude, I haven't seen a puppy."

Suddenly, the little boy jumped up and down, shouting and pointing to something behind Tommy: "Puppy, puppy, I see the puppy!"

Still crouching, Tommy turned around and stared up into the eyes of a giant-sized dog only inches from his face. The dog's huge tongue licked and slobbered excitedly as Tommy fell backward until he was on his back and the dog was now standing over him. The little boy laughed and laughed.

"That's the puppy?" Tommy asked still lying on the damp floor and trying to cover his face with his arms.

William smiled and said, "That's what they call him. He's actually a giant mastiff. And there's another dog, a spaniel. Two dogs and a hundred and two passengers."

Other children joined the first little boy and they all started petting the dog. It was large enough that the smallest of the children could probably ride it like a horse.

I leaned over to help Tommy to his feet. He grabbed my hand and while hoisting him up I forgot about the low ceiling. "Ouch," I said.

"It takes some getting used to," said William. "Are you all right?"

"I'll be fine. No worries." I could already feel the raised bump on the top of my head.

"The *Mayflower* was not built to be a passenger ship. It's a cargo ship. However, as you can see we've converted this crawl-space into our living quarters," said William.

I looked around and could vaguely see that many passengers were lying down on rugs or sitting on chairs, chests of clothing, or leaning up against casks that were probably filled with water or beer. Many looked seasick, with chamber pots close by in case they had to vomit.

Tommy turned to one of the children who were petting the dog and asked, "Do you have to stay down here all the time?"

"Not all of the time," said a girl who was about eight years old. "Only when the wind is really pushy and the waves are really big."

"The waves don't feel really big from down here," Tommy said.

Overhearing the conversation, William crouched down to his knees and spoke to all of the children, including Tommy. "It's true that this deck can be very deceiving about what's happening outside. But the *Mayflower* is a special kind of ship. Have you ever seen a duck float on top of the waves? It just sits there, perfectly balanced while easily floating up and over and around the water. Well, the *Mayflower* is like a duck." William reached out and while gently pressing against a little boy's nose he made the noise "quack, quack." The children laughed.

A young teenage boy who was standing nearby raised his hand and said, "I haven't seen a duck, but I have seen a seagull. Or at least I think it was a seagull. I'm not sure because I didn't see it float very long before a giant shark three times the size of the *Mayflower* jumped out of the water and ate the whole thing in one gulp."

"It's true," said a second boy, about the same age as the first. They looked like brothers. "I saw the same shark. In fact, I saw it following the *Mayflower* just a few minutes ago."

The young children stood there looking horrified, their eyes nearly as big as their opened mouths.

"D-d-did you really see such a shark?" a little girl finally asked.

"No, he did not!" said a man coming from behind the two teenage boys. Although it was dark, I could tell that he was shorter than William but probably close to the same age, maybe a little older. He looked like a strong man with broad shoulders. His red beard and mustache were neatly trimmed and he wore fine clothing, with a sword hanging from his side. I could see Tommy's eyes fixed on the sword.

He grabbed the ears of both of the teenage boys and forced them to their knees. He spoke with authority and while twisting their ears he said, "I warned you Billington boys. I told you I wouldn't put up with your nonsense. You will now tell these children the truth."

Painfully, the boys spoke as fast as they could. "We didn't see a shark." "Ouch, or a seagull." "We're sorry for scaring you." "Ow, it was just a fib." "We were just teasing you." "That really hurts, it won't happen again. . . ."

"Thank you, Captain Standish, that will be enough," said William Bradford.

Like two fish being released in a shallow pool, the boys darted for the other side of the darkened ship.

"Let me introduce you to Captain Myles Standish," said William. "Captain Standish was with us in Holland. He will be handling our colony's military matters in America."

Tommy leaned close to me and whispered, "I'm glad he's not our substitute teacher. He doesn't mess around. My friend's dad was in the military, and let's just say no one wanted to get on his bad side. Captain Standish seems stricter than Principal Sherman."

We exchanged introductions and Tommy immediately asked, "Will you teach me how to fight with a sword?"

"I'd be delighted," said Myles, "but ear-twisting can also be very effective." He winked and smiled while messing up Tommy's hair. "When the weather gets better I can teach you the art of swordfighting on the upper deck."

William asked Myles, "Have you seen Elder Brewster?"

"I believe he's returned to the captain's cabin to—"

Before Myles could finish his sentence a loud bell started to ring. "Ding, ding. Ding, ding. Ding, ding." Through the open hatch we heard someone shout, "Man overboard!"

As we hurried to follow William and Myles back to the hatch and up the ladder, I noticed several families calling out for sons and daughters, husbands and wives. Like a hen rushing to gather her chicks, fathers and mothers were frantically searching for their own children, hoping whoever went overboard wasn't one of their own.

We rushed up the ladder, through the hatch, and onto the upper deck. It was like we landed on a different planet. Although it was much brighter and the air much fresher, the wind was howling through the ropes and rigging, and giant waves looked like they could smother the *Mayflower* at any moment. We were drenched from the water spraying in every direction. We scrambled toward several sailors shouting and pointing at something in the water.

"He fell over the ship's railing right there!" a sailor shouted.

An older man was barking orders to the crew and I assumed he must be the captain of the *Mayflower*. He was wearing a long coat with a stocking cap similar to what the sailors were wearing.

William called to the older man, "Captain Jones, look over there!" He pointed to a rope attached to the upper sail. "It looks like it's dragging something."

The captain looked doubtful but in a split second yelled at the crew, "Get that topsail halyard out of the water!"

I studied the end of the rope that was lost in the waves behind us. For a few seconds, I saw something that looked like a body lift up out of the water and then become consumed again by another wave.

"A man!" I shouted. "He's hanging on to the end of that rope." I wasn't 100 percent sure but I believed William Bradford's suspicion was correct.

"He's caught in the rope. He's already dead!" shouted a sailor. "Leave him for the sharks."

"I give the orders around here, sailor!" shouted Captain Jones. "Get that halyard out of the water! And that man still better be on the end of it or I wouldn't want to be you!"

Captain Jones's voice was so loud and so threatening that the crew looked more afraid of the captain than they did of the storm. Within seconds they had the rope and began pulling with all their might. "Heave, heave, heave!" they shouted in unison.

It felt like buckets of water were being thrown on us from every direction. The ship rocked again and again. It was almost impossible to stand up without holding on to something. I tried to keep my eye on the end of the rope that the sailors were hauling in, and hoped to spot the dangling body, but I slipped and slid across the width of the twenty-five-foot deck. It might have been fun if I were at a water park. As I looked back to where I was standing, I saw that William had joined the sailors and was pulling the rope as well. Tommy was on his hands and knees nearly twenty feet away. He was dangerously close to the railing and as he attempted to stand the boat suddenly lurched leeward. Helplessly, I saw Tommy slip and tip over the ship's railing headfirst. I scrambled toward Tommy but realized I just wasn't close enough to help him. Fortunately, Myles Standish was. He reached over and grabbed Tommy's right leg in the nick of time. Just as Myles was slipping, I reached out and grabbed his arm as he continued to pull Tommy back onto the ship.

"I'm taking the boy to the captain's cabin! You should come, too!" shouted Myles.

"Thank you, Captain Standish!" I yelled, not fully realizing

An artist's rendering of William Brewster.

An artist's rendering of Myles Standish.

the gravity of what had just happened. "I'll follow you in just a minute!" I wanted to witness the rescue of the man in the water.

I yelled to Tommy, "Go with Captain Standish! I'll be right behind you!"

The sailors continued to heave and pull the rope in rhythm. The end of the rope was nearing the rudder. It reached the aft of the ship and then the hull. Without question, there was a man hanging on to the end of that rope with fierce desperation.

"Grab a boat hook!" shouted Captain Jones. "Haul him up and snag him with the hook!"

After several more minutes, the man was hauled back into the boat. He rolled to his side and coughed up seawater.

"Take him to my cabin!" the captain ordered.

Two sailors pulled the man to his feet. They helped him up the ladder to the quarterdeck and into the captain's cabin.

"He's lucky to be alive," I said as I patted William on the back.

"Not luck," William said. "It's a miracle. Surely, this is a divine sign. We will ask Elder Brewster. Whenever there is doubt or fear among the passengers we can always turn to him for guidance and strength. He has great wisdom and spiritual strength." As William opened the door to the captain's cabin he turned back and said, "Elder Brewster always provides a sense of calm in troubled times. I'm eager for you to meet him."

"Did I hear my name? Am I needed?" asked a man dressed in a long blue robe. His high collar and stately appearance reminded me of someone of religious authority. He had kind eyes and his peppered hair was thin and receding. He was sitting across from Myles Standish and Tommy. They all stood and rushed over to us when they saw the sailors help the stumbling man to a bed.

"Elder Brewster," said William. "John Howland fell overboard but was saved."

"If he had followed the rules and stayed below deck during a storm he wouldn't look like a drowned rat," said Myles.

"You say he fell overboard?" asked Elder Brewster, sounding greatly concerned. "And yet he is back on the ship? Tell me what happened."

William explained all that had happened.

"Extraordinary," said Elder Brewster.

John started coughing again. He breathed deeply as his eyes scanned the room. "I can't believe . . . I'm alive. . . . Thank you for saving me."

"John, my dear boy, what were you doing on the upper deck during a tempest?" asked Elder Brewster.

Breathlessly, John replied, "I'm sorry. Truly, I am. I was sitting in my space down below in the tween deck. The passengers next to me were seasick and both threw up in their chamber pots. The stench was more than I could handle. I just needed some fresh air. I felt the walls of the ship's hull closing in all around me, and down below it didn't feel like the weather was a raging tempest. So I climbed the ladder as fast as I could, opened the hatch, and jumped out only to find that I had entered a terrible fury."

"Do not condemn yourself, John," said Elder Brewster. "Your salvation from certain death is a miraculous sign. Everything happens for a reason. God has chosen to save you, which I believe means we are certain to make it to America."

William looked at me and nodded in agreement.

The wind blew in as Captain Jones entered his cabin and removed his heavy coat. I guessed he was fifty years old. His hair and beard were gray. He wore a blue stocking cap like the other sailors but his clothing was cleaner and more distinguished. He said, "I'm sorry for my delay. How is the passenger?"

"He's alive," said William.

"He's welcome to stay here until he fully recovers," said Captain Jones.

William approached the captain and said, "I want to personally thank you for acting quickly and ordering your men to do the same. It's apparent your crew respects you."

Captain Jones laughed, "Ha, they respect me or fear me. Either way, it got the job done. But I warn you, there are sailors on this ship that would rather see all of the Puritans fed to the sharks."

"We are used to being bullied and threatened, Captain Jones," William said.

"Rest assured," said Elder Brewster, "we will not retaliate. God will smite those who afflict the righteous, just as he saves those who are good and true."

I thought about the sailor who already threatened me, twice. I believed the warning from Captain Jones. But I wondered if the captain believed the words of Elder Brewster.

As the captain talked to the other Pilgrim leaders, Tommy walked over to John's bed and said, "Dude, I can't believe you hung on to that rope. That was amazing! You're like the seventeenth-century version of Chuck Norris."

John looked at Tommy, confused. "My name is John Howland. I know not anyone named Dude, but apparently you mistake me for some stranger by that name. And I know not of any Chuck Norris. But it sounded like a compliment, so thank you."

William introduced me to both Captain Christopher Jones and Elder William Brewster, the current religious leader of the

Puritans. They invited Tommy and me to stay in the captain's cabin until the storm blew over. While we waited, Captain Jones offered us some salted beef.

"This is pretty good," Tommy said, chewing. "It's just like beef jerky."

"Jerky?" Myles questioned. "I'm not familiar with that word."

Still chewing, I butted in and said, "Oh, it's an old family recipe."

As we finished our sticks of salted beef, I walked over to William and said, "I just wanted to say that I think you make a fine leader."

William said, "Thank you, Rush Revere. I'm not sure about being a fine leader. I just do what needs to be done."

"Even if it means risking your own life?" I asked.

"I would risk my life to do the right thing every time. When I was a young boy I became very ill. I had to stay at home. I had time to read many books, especially the Bible. I promised God that I would try my best to make the right choice every time. I am far from being perfect. My wife will tell you that," William said with a smile. "But I will do everything I can to help make our colony, our New World, our land of America a place where religious freedom comes first. If we can become a nation under God and put our trust in Him, I believe we shall prosper."

I pondered those words and realized how important they would be to our Founding Fathers.

The ocean settled sooner than I expected. It was still drizzling outside but I realized it would be a good time to find Liberty, before the upper deck got too crowded. We thanked our guests and excused ourselves.

"I hope Liberty is okay," Tommy said.

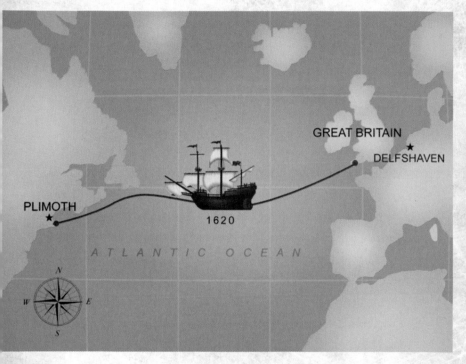

Route of the *Mayflower*, 1620.

We walked across the quarterdeck, down the ladder, and to the door of the capstan room. We opened it and found Liberty wedged between a side wall and the wooden levers of the capstan, sleeping peacefully.

"Liberty," Tommy said.

Nothing.

"Liberty!" Tommy shouted.

Still nothing.

"Here, let me try," I said. I opened Liberty's saddlebag and pulled out an apple that we had picked in Holland. I waved it in front of Liberty's nose.

With his eyes still closed, Liberty wrapped his lips around the apple and chewed heartily. I grabbed several more apples and fed them to him one by one. He kept his eyes closed while he chewed and said, "I must have taken a nap. Ships always do that to me. The more the rocking the more tired I become. Did I miss anything?"

"Nothing too important," I said, still feeding him the apples. "But it's time to jump forward to the end of the *Mayflower* voyage. There's a new land to discover! There are Indians to befriend and a new colony to build. And a celebration to be had called Thanksgiving!"

Liberty's eyes popped open and said, "Thanksgiving! Pumpkin pie. Cranberries. Squash and green beans and carrots and corn and peas and those miniature pumpkins! Now you're speaking my language! What are we waiting for?" With a burst of energy he walked out onto the open deck and vanished into thin air.

"What we need now is a distraction so Liberty can create the time portal and we can jump through it," I said. "Anyone have an idea?"

"Whoa, is that a real whale?" Tommy said while pointing starboard, off the bow of the ship.

"Very convincing, Tommy," I said. "You're a very good actor. Now we just have to convince everyone else on deck."

"I'm not kidding, look!" Tommy said.

I turned around and, sure enough, a giant sperm whale nearly sixty feet long surfaced the water. And not just one, but several whales. An entire pod of sperm whales was just two hundred yards off the starboard bow. Sailors called to each other and pointed in the direction of the whales.

"Quickly, now's our chance. To the opposite side of the ship!" I whispered.

The diversion worked. Liberty reappeared and we slipped onto his back. Liberty said, *"Rush, rush, rushing to history!"*

I echoed his words with "November ninth, 1620, the *Mayflower*." Nobody noticed as we jumped through the time portal.

Chapter 5

arkness concealed our return to the *Mayflower's* upper deck. However, the sun was close to rising and would soon stretch its rays across the eastern horizon. A light breeze drifted across our faces, reminding us that winter was just around the corner. We appeared to have landed on the ship we left from, except instead of September it was now November. It was still too dark to see much, but I was worried about the condition of the passengers and crew. I knew they lacked food and water. I knew they lacked good nutrition, particularly vitamin C, in their diet. Certainly, this would cause many to suffer from scurvy—a disease known to cause swollen and bleeding gums and ultimately, death. And, most important, I knew they lacked hope. For days and weeks the Pilgrims hoped that they would find land. They hoped for an end to the miserable conditions they had to endure. Now, after suffering for two months, there was still no sign of dry ground. Even I could feel the grip of hopelessness trying to strangle me. I quickly turned to Liberty and Tommy in an effort to break the despair I was feeling.

"Nice jumping, Liberty," I said, scratching him behind the ear.

"Aw, shucks! I bet you say that to all the magical horses who leap you across the Atlantic Ocean," Liberty said, grinning.

Tommy jumped off Liberty's saddle and said, "Hey, if there are other horses like you, I want one!"

Curious, I asked, "If you had a horse like Liberty, what exceptional event in American history would you visit first?"

"Hmm," Tommy thought, "that's a tough one. Probably 1969, when Apollo 11 launched into space and Neil Armstrong became the first man to set foot on the moon. That would be awesome!"

"Oh, I remember watching that on television," said Liberty. "When he landed on the moon he said, 'That's one small step for man, one giant leap for mankind.' Although, personally, I think a giant leap through time is more impressive."

"Wait, you mean that if you wanted to you could time-jump to the moon?" Tommy asked.

"Well, if a cow can jump over the moon, certainly a horse can!" Liberty huffed.

"All right, kids," I intervened. "Let's get back to business. It's almost light enough now to see what's happening on the ship. In fact, I think that's Captain Jones and William Bradford up on the poop deck."

Tommy burst out laughing and asked, "Did you just say 'poop' deck?"

Then Liberty started laughing. "It's funny when you say it like that! Poop deck. Poop deck."

I rolled my eyes and waited until the two of them stopped laughing. "Are you finished? Honestly, you're acting like a couple of five-year-olds."

"Um, actually," Liberty tried to say, "I *am* five."

Then they both started laughing again. In fact, watching them laugh made me start to laugh.

"For the record," I said, smiling, "the 'poop' deck is the deck above the captain's cabin, built in the rear or stern of the ship. I believe the name originates from the French word for stern, *la poupe*."

More laughter. Tommy and Liberty were leaning on each other now, laughing hysterically, and saying in their best French accent, "La poupe, la poupe."

"Liberty," I said, "I think you better disappear and hide yourself in the capstan room. I think someone is approaching." Instantly, Liberty vanished as we heard a familiar voice say, "I'm glad to see someone can laugh under the circumstances. Who goes there and why all the frivolity?"

As the voice got closer we saw Myles Standish, his sword still hanging from his side. His clothes were haggard and he smelled like he hadn't bathed in days or weeks or even a couple of months. However, despite his appearance he was smiling.

"Hi, Captain Standish," said Tommy, standing up straight.

"Oh, hello, Tommy. Hello, Rush. I was thinking about you just the other day. I'd meant to come find you but with all my duties I'm afraid I've not been very attentive. I must say it's good to see you in such fine spirits. Hearing you laugh put a smile on my face. I can't remember the last time I smiled. Thank you for that," said Myles.

"It appears our laughter may be contagious," I said.

"Let's hope it spreads quickly. Our people are beginning to doubt. Elder Brewster is encouraging as many as he can. He reminds us to pray day and night. But so many are sick. We are nearly out of water, and we have little food. We've had much contention and despair among the passengers and crew. Thankfully, the cruelest of them is no longer with us."

"Did someone die?" asked Tommy.

"Yes, lad. We've kept it quiet because we didn't want to worry the rest of you below deck. Many days ago one of the sailors, a vile, profane, and arrogant man, was stricken with disease and died in a wretched way."

A thought occurred to me and I asked, "I remember one sailor with a scar above his cheek. He was heartless about our seasickness and threatened to feed all the Puritans to the sharks. Was it him?"

Myles nodded. "The very one," he said. "That sailor mocked our suffering and cursed our people endlessly. He swore and hoped to cast half of us overboard before we came to our journey's end. Yet he himself was the first to be thrown overboard. The word has spread that it was the just hand of God who did it."

Tommy raised his hand as if he were in the classroom and asked, "Captain Standish, what happens when people get sick on the *Mayflower*? Is there a doctor's office on the boat?"

"No, Tommy, not really," said Myles. "We have people who care for the sick but there isn't much that can be done when the illness is severe."

"Do you ever feel like you want to give up and go back to Holland?" asked Tommy.

"No, son," Myles said, firmly. "Abandoning this voyage is out of the question, at least for me. We must go on despite the hardships. If we give up now, we will never know what land is ahead. If we turn this vessel around, we will be back to a place where we cannot really be free."

"Do you think the king would put all of you in jail?"

"Perhaps," said Myles, "even if we made it back to Holland without anyone knowing, we couldn't go to our own church. The Church of England would tell us how we must act and how we must think."

Tommy's brow was furrowed as he thought about what Myles had said. "Yeah, I don't like when people try to control me. My mom always tells me to think for myself and not just follow the crowd. She says I should stand up for what I believe even if it's not popular."

"It sounds like you have a very smart mother," said Myles.

"Yeah, and she's also really strict about me doing my chores around the house. You'd probably really like her."

Myles laughed and said, "You are an incredibly bright boy, Tommy. I'm glad you are here. You fit in perfectly with our mission.

"Come, Rush Revere and Tommy," he said. "Let me take you to Captain Jones and William. He's navigating the ship from the poop deck."

I gave Tommy "the look."

Both of Tommy's hands went into the air. "Hey, the joke's over for me. That was so 1620," he said, winking.

As we walked to visit with Captain Jones and William, Tommy said, "Captain Standish, I never really got a chance to thank you for, you know, the way you caught me. I mean, you

Mayflower in rough seas, 1620.

were lightning fast. And then how you lifted me up by my leg. You were like the Hulk. Anyway, thanks for saving my life."

Myles stopped and looked at Tommy. He finally said, "Tommy, I don't know if I'm any stronger or faster than any other man. But if I've learned anything while living among the Puritans it's that everything happens for a reason. Simply, you weren't supposed to fall off this ship. It wasn't your time."

Boy, is that the truth, I thought.

Myles continued: "I'm glad I was standing next to you when you fell overboard. I'm glad I could save you. But my part in helping you is over and yours has just begun. Think of it as a second chance. What will you do with your life now that you couldn't have done if I hadn't caught you?"

"Wow, that's deep. But I get it," said Tommy.

"Good," said Myles. "Go do something great with your life, Tommy. We'll talk more soon. And your first sword lesson begins when we get to dry ground! A man is always better off when he knows how to protect himself and his family!" Myles turned to leave, but then stopped with a quizzical look and asked, "Did you say I was like the Hulk? Who or what is the Hulk?"

Tommy paused for just a second and replied, "Oh, well, he's just this guy back home. Sort of a hero. He's really strong and pretty much invincible."

"Thank you for the compliment. I think I would like to meet this Hulk someday," Myles said, smiling. He then turned on his heel and headed for the ladder.

When Captain Jones and William Bradford saw us, William said, "Rush Revere! Please forgive my neglect. It's good to see you. I assume you've been surviving with the others below deck? I know I shouldn't assume but with so many passengers suffering from seasickness, including my wife, I've found myself unable to visit everyone I'd like."

"No worries," I said. "Tommy and I are definitely surviving and feeling very optimistic today!"

I noticed Captain Jones held a three-foot-long stick on which was attached a sliding crosspiece. I assumed it was sort of a compass. That's when Tommy asked, "What's that in your hand?"

"It's a cross-staff," said Captain Jones. "It helps me know where to steer the ship. I place it up to my eye and measure the distance between a star, the moon, or the sun and the horizon. It helps me calculate the ship's position. But with all the bad weather it's been difficult to know for sure how far we are from land."

Curious, I asked, "And where are we supposed to be by now?"

"By now I expected us to be at the Jamestown Settlement on the Hudson River." At that point in history, the Jamestown settlement extended all the way up the mid-Atlantic coast to what is now New York. "But with all the storms it looks like we have traveled much farther north than I expected," said the Captain.

Tommy whispered to me, "Too bad they didn't have a GPS."

William added, "By Captain Jones's calculations we should spot land in a day or so."

"Look," said Tommy, pointing up into the morning sky. "Isn't that a seagull? And there's another! I'm pretty sure those seagulls are coastal birds."

In the moment Tommy finished speaking we heard a sailor shout from above, "Land, ho!"

Passengers started streaming out from the hatches that led to the tween deck. Many were lifted and helped up the ladder, too sick or weary to walk on their own. Their expressions were mixed between hope and doubt as if they couldn't believe their ears. The bow of the ship pointed westward as all eyes raced to see what they hadn't seen for more than two months. Land! Sure enough, a distant strip of land could be seen on the horizon. As soon as the Pilgrims on the upper deck saw the outline of dry ground, they fell to their knees and began to weep. Others shouted for joy and almost everyone found someone to hug. Elder Brewster called the Saints together, and even some of the Strangers came, and together they offered a word a prayer. They knelt to give thanks to God for persevering and protecting them. After they prayed, they sang a hymn. Some were too emotional to sing as they watched the approaching land and simply cried tears of relief. Even the sick and weary looked to have renewed health and strength.

I noticed William had a giant smile on his face and what looked to be a tear in his eye. He said, "We left Plymouth, England, on September sixth and today is . . ."

"November ninth," Tommy finished. "You've been sailing straight for sixty-five days!"

"Very good, Tommy," said Captain Jones. "And many of the passengers have been seasick for all sixty-five days."

William breathed deeply and nearly laughed when he said, "They are not feeling sick now. They are exceedingly happy and grateful that God has preserved us over this vast and furious ocean."

"And it looks like a beautiful day," I said. "Soon we'll be on dry ground."

"Yes," the Captain agreed, "but remember, we are far north of our original destination. We were supposed to land at the Hudson River. Instead, it appears we are headed toward New England—Cape Cod, to be exact."

"It is needful that we find our way to the coast as fast as

possible," said William. "Our provisions are low and many passengers are sick and even diseased."

"We sail by the wind," said Captain Jones. "Right now, the wind is coming from the north. We'll sail to the coast and follow the coastline swiftly to the Hudson River."

They all agreed and soon a colony of seagulls flew overhead, welcoming the *Mayflower* as it drifted out of deep blue waters and into emerald green. Passengers crowded the starboard side of the ship and watched with keen interest at the thick forest of trees and bushes with orange and yellow leaves that grew beyond the empty beaches.

I watched these remarkable passengers, amazed at how genuinely tough they were. The kind of hardship they experienced on the *Mayflower* is something that modern-day people will seldom, if ever, experience. And yet these Pilgrims did it with gusto! They hadn't been spoiled by wall-to-wall carpets, central heating, and microwave ovens. They lived and endured hard things because that is just how it was. And so they passed the first test. The next would be the building of a new colony. I knew it wouldn't be easy, but I was sure that these rugged individuals would, again, find a way to overcome any trial.

Myles Standish walked up to us and asked, "What catches your eye out there, Tommy?" Tommy gripped the railing as he stared at the passing wilderness. "Oh, well, I was just wondering what might be in those woods," he said, sounding a little bit nervous.

Myles answered, "All the things that will sustain us. Wood, berries, animals, water, and soil."

"And Indians?" asked Tommy.

"Yes, probably Indians," Myles said. "We will do what we must to protect ourselves. We have swords and muskets and cannons if need be."

"That's good to know," said Tommy.

"Hopefully, we won't have to use them," said William.

As I looked ahead along the coast I wondered if Captain Jones had ever sailed these waters. Surely, every coastline is different and there's always a chance of hidden dangers.

Suddenly, a sailor yelled from above, "Shoals ahead! Turn port side!"

"Aren't shoals like a sandbank or sandbar out in the open water?" Tommy asked.

"Yes," I said to Tommy softly. "And if I'm not mistaken this place is called Pollock Rip—it's a ship's graveyard. If the captain doesn't avoid the shoals the *Mayflower* could get pinned or even shipwrecked. A direct hit could smash the ship's hull."

Waves crashed against the shoals as water swirled up and over the threatening sandbars. The wind died down to almost nothing but the *Mayflower* drifted dangerously closer to the roaring breakers.

"We are in great danger!" said Captain Jones with urgency. His eyes were fixed on the shoals ahead. "A southern wind would be especially helpful right now!"

Calmly, William said, "We've not come this far to shipwreck now. What must we do?"

"Watch for shoals," said Captain Jones. "And keep your people away from my sailors so they can do their jobs."

"With God all things are possible," said Elder Brewster from behind me.

I turned and asked, "Do you have any counsel, any advice?"

"Pray," he said, smiling. "God will make up the difference. He created the heavens and the earth. Surely, He can steer a ship to safety."

Remarkably, the wind began to blow, a southern wind! The sails shifted and the *Mayflower* turned just in time, missing the shoals by only a few feet.

"I'm afraid we won't be landing at the Hudson River. This coastline is too dangerous," said Captain Jones. "Now that the wind has changed directions our best chance is to sail north, back around Cape Cod to New England."

William gave a worried look at Myles, who said, "The Strangers will not like it."

William looked deep in thought and said, "Yes, the Strangers will insist we land at the Hudson."

"Then they can jump off my ship and swim if they want to," said Captain Jones. "I will go and explain to them the situation. I will not have a mutiny on my ship."

"Captain Standish and I will go with you," said William. "Rush and Tommy, you're welcome to come but please don't feel like you have to."

I eagerly replied, "We're right behind you. If there's anything you need, just ask."

"Thank you, Rush Revere, for all the support you've given."

We climbed down from the poop deck to the quarterdeck and then climbed down again to the upper deck. Several passengers climbed up from the tween deck. Liberty was waiting for us on the upper deck.

As Myles predicted, the Strangers were in an uproar when they heard the news. Shouts could be heard from above and below deck. It sounded like a mob. Children were crying and even the giant mastiff was barking at everyone and everything.

Hourglass used to tell time on the voyage.

Compass dial with lid used to navigate during the day.

Compass and sundial made of silver, ivory, brass, and glass used to tell time during the day.

A nocturnal, an instrument that uses the stars to tell the time at night.

Portable telescope used to view at a distance.

A jack screw similar to this raised houses in Plymouth and saved the *Mayflower* from sinking.

"Please," pleaded William, trying to calm both Stranger and Saint. "I'm sure we can work this out. We've shared the same boat for sixty-five days. We've had our differences but we've come to know each other. We've both suffered and survived together. We've shared our provisions and our stories and our dreams knowing that we, all of us, would be a new colony."

Captain Jones added, "I've seen firsthand how Saint and Stranger have worked together for the good of all. When we were mid-ocean and that monstrous wave cracked one of the ship's core beams, I witnessed how you rallied to find a solution. In desperation, you collectively used a screw jack to help my carpenter repair the fractured beam."

One of the Strangers stepped forward and raised his hands to speak.

"Who is that?" Tommy asked. "Is he a Stranger or a Saint?"

Myles leaned over to us and whispered, "That's Stephen Hopkins, a Stranger. His wife gave birth to a baby boy during our voyage. They named him Oceanus."

Tommy raised his eyebrows and whispered back, "Oceanus?"

Myles shrugged his shoulders and smirked.

"It's an odd name, for sure," I said, "But when the other kids ask him about it he can always say, 'It's because I was born aboard the *Mayflower.*'"

"Yeah," Tommy agreed, "not many people can say that."

Stephen Hopkins spoke boldly: "We agreed to help and use the screw jack because we all had a common goal. We all agreed to settle at the Hudson River. And now we're headed in the opposite direction." He pointed at William Bradford, Myles Standish, Elder Brewster, and the other Puritan members and shouted, "Land where you want, but when we come ashore we'll use our own liberty, for none have the power to command us!"

"Did he just say they'll use their own horse named Liberty?" whispered Liberty. "What are the odds that there are two horses with the same name on the same ship?"

"They weren't referring to a different horse, they said—"

Liberty interrupted: "Well, if they think they're going to use me they better think again. I'm not another man's property. I mean, I used to be but that was in the eighteenth century and just because we're in the seventeenth century doesn't mean I'm going to give up my twenty-first-century freedoms."

Liberty's mouth was so close to my face that his whiskers tickled my ear. I whispered back, "Nobody is going to use you. They might as well try to tame a thousand wild horses with nothing but a whistle."

"Shh," Liberty hushed. "I'm trying to listen to what's happening."

I resisted the urge to strangle my horse and continued listening.

William said, "I understand your frustration. I do. We all have advantages by settling at the Hudson River. However, right now that's not an option. The truth is the only way for this new colony to succeed financially is if we all stay together and work together."

Stephen Hopkins turned to discuss the matter with his fellow Strangers. Before long, they reluctantly agreed that a union with the Saints or Puritans was important for the colony to survive and thrive.

William turned to Captain Jones and said, "Captain, I request that we set anchor at Cape Cod so that we might compose an agreement, something that would bind us all together." He turned to the large crowd of passengers on the upper deck and continued: "We need a document that will help create just and equal laws in our new colony. We'll need a government and a governor, but more important, we must choose this by common consent where majority rules. Once this agreement is composed, I propose that we sign it as a promise to obey and support the rules and laws which we agree to."

I whispered to Tommy, "This is a key moment of American history. The agreement that William Bradford is proposing is the Mayflower Compact. It is said to be just as important to American history as the Declaration of Independence."

The passengers agreed to creating the agreement and Captain Jones offered William Bradford his personal cabin and desk to compose the agreement.

I approached William and said, "That was a difficult situation but you handled it well."

"Thank you," said William. "It was the mutinous speeches that made me determined to find a solution."

"And what are you thinking this agreement will do?" I asked.

"It's a good question. By signing this agreement everyone on this ship is agreeing, when we land, to live and work together so that we can survive. It will be a brief outline of self-government. We'll still profess our allegiance to King James but we also need just and equal laws suited to our new settlement and new way of life. We are far from England and so we must do what is convenient for the general good of the colony."

"That is really ingenious," I said.

Signing of the Mayflower Compact on board the *Mayflower* in 1620.

IN the Name of God, Amen. We whose Names are under-written, the Loyal Subjects of our dread Soveraign Lord King *James*, by the grace of God of *Great Britain*, *France* and *Ireland*, King, *Defendor of the Faith*, *&c.* Having undertaken for the glory of God, and advancement of the Christian Faith, and the Honour of our King and Countrey, a Voyage to plant the first Colony in the Northern parts of *Virginia* ; Do by these Presents solemnly and mutually, in the presence of God and one another, Covenant and Combine our selves together into a Civil Body Politick, for our better ordering and preservation, and furtherance of the ends aforesaid : and by virtue hereof do enact, constitute and frame such just and equal Laws, O dinances, Acts, Constitutions and Officers, from time to time, as shall be thought most meet and convenient for the general good of the Colony ; unto which we promise all due submission and obedience. In witness whereof we have hereunto subscribed our Names at *Cape Cod*, the eleventh of *November*, in the Reign of our Soveraign Lord King *James*, of *England*, *France* and *Ireland* the eighteenth, and of *Scotland* the fifty fourth, *Anno Dom.* 1610.

John Carver.
William Bradford.
Edward Winslow.
William Brewster.
Isaac Allerton.
Miles Standish.
John Alden. —

Samuel Fuller.
Christopher Martin.
William Mullins.
William White.
Richard Warren.
John Howland.
Steven Hopkins.

Edward Tilly.
John Tilly.
Francis Cook.
Thomas Rogers.
Thomas Tinker.
John Ridgdale.
Edward Fuller.
John

Mayflower Compact, establishing the rule of fairness under law in Plymouth Colony, signed by almost all men on board the *Mayflower*.

Signatures of several Mayflower Compact signers, including William Brewster, Myles Standish, and William Bradford.

"If we can get everyone to agree it will be," William said with a chuckle.

I patted him on the back and said, "I predict that this very agreement you're proposing will be referred to by many English colonists who will settle in America in the years to come. In fact, it might very well be the beginning of a greater constitution for all Americans."

"You are always thinking of the future, Rush Revere," said William, smiling. "I like that about you. If you'll excuse me, I have some writing to do."

William and several other passengers climbed the stairs to the captain's cabin.

"I love happy endings," whispered Liberty.

"Ending?" I said. "Liberty, this is just the start. In a way, this is like Neil Armstrong landing on the moon."

"It is?" Tommy questioned.

"Absolutely! The Pilgrims may not be the first to discover the New World but their footprint in New England will eventually lead to the making of the United States of America."

"Wow," Tommy said. "I never thought of it like that."

"It's hard for me to think about anything with an empty stomach," said Liberty.

I grabbed a few more apples out of Liberty's saddlebag and fed them to him. Tommy and I ate an apple as well.

When we finished Tommy asked, "Hey, do you think we could climb up and watch them sign the Mayflower Compact?"

"You took the words right out of my mouth," I said.

"Don't worry about me," Liberty sighed, obviously trying to make us feel guilty for leaving him. "You're off to watch one of the most important events in American history while the rest of us get stuck out in the cold. It reminds me of that one Christmas reindeer. . . ."

"Rudolph?" Tommy said.

"Yes! Rudolph, the red-nosed reindeer. He wanted to join in the reindeer games, but the other reindeer wouldn't let him."

"How thoughtless of me," I said. "You're absolutely right. We should be filming this so I can use it as a teaching moment back in class."

"Um, well, that's not exactly what I . . . ," Liberty tried to say.

I added, "And I'll find you the biggest and juiciest carrots when we get home. Deal?" I asked.

"All right," Liberty sighed. "I suppose nothing says I love you and I forgive you and I'll make sure I include you the next time like a big, juicy carrot. Or a fresh head of cabbage. Or large, crisp turnips. And I'm especially fond of cauliflower. . . ."

While Liberty continued daydreaming I whispered to Tommy, "Let's go."

When we reached the quarterdeck to the captain's cabin, we turned to wave at Liberty, who looked deep in thought.

We shuffled into the crowded room as many Saints and Strangers surrounded the captain's desk, where William Bradford was sitting and composing the agreement. Most men were standing but Myles Standish sat close by William. Myles wore his breastplate and helmet and looked as if he was ready to pounce upon anyone who objected to William's composition. Overall, the room had a peaceful mood. Finally, William dipped the quill into the inkwell and signed his name at the bottom. He dipped the quill again and handed it to Myles Standish, who signed his name. One by one, the men in the room began signing their names. As men exited the cabin, other men entered to sign their names.

As the signing continued, Tommy whispered, "Try taking my picture with your smartphone. I'll squeeze my way in so you can get me by the Mayflower Compact, okay?"

"I'll do my best," I said.

Tommy squirmed his way to the table and then stood on his tiptoes, smiling a big cheesy grin. I stood at the back of the room, removed my phone from my pocket, and as discreetly as possible took a picture of Tommy's first event in American history.

When Tommy made it back to me he said, "We should go and get Freedom. I feel bad that she hasn't been here to see all of this. I don't want her to miss the Pilgrims' landing."

"Good idea," I said. "We'll slip away before anyone notices."

We exited the captain's cabin and climbed down the ladder to the upper deck, but when we looked inside the capstan room for Liberty he wasn't there. That's odd, I thought.

"There he is," Tommy said, pointing to the far side of the ship. For an instant, Liberty appeared and then disappeared. What was he doing? I wondered.

We quickly walked over to where we had last seen him and whispered, "Liberty! What are you doing?"

Liberty reappeared right next to us. Pointing at the hatch that led to the tween deck he said, "Something fishy is going on down there, and I'm not talking about fish. I watched two teenage boys who looked very mischievous climb down this ladder and say something about shooting off a musket. I have a bad feeling about this."

"I'll go check it out," said Tommy. "I'll let you know what I see."

I paused to think about whether or not that was such a good idea. Finally, I said, "All right, but just take a look and then come right back up and tell us what you see."

Quick as a cat, Tommy sprang down the ladder. After a couple of minutes his head popped up and he said, "It's the Billington boys. You know, those teenagers that Myles scolded for scaring those little kids with that shark story. They're playing with their dad's musket. I think they're going to try to shoot it."

"That doesn't sound good," I said.

"Yeah, and it gets worse. I noticed they're sitting near a barrel of gunpowder. If the gun ignites the gunpowder . . . ," Tommy said, assuming we knew how his sentence would end.

"Ka-boom," said Liberty. "Neil Armstrong won't be the first man on the moon. The Billington boys will be."

"Tommy, run and get Myles," I said. "I'll climb down and try to stop them."

Before either Tommy or I moved, we heard a loud musket blast from the deck below. Immediately, Liberty took a deep breath and disappeared. We waited two more seconds and were relieved when the rest of the ship didn't blow up. Instantly, the captain's door swung open and several men streamed out of the cabin, including Captain Jones.

"Who fired that musket?!" the captain yelled.

Tommy and I pointed to the hatch that led to the tween deck.

I whispered to Tommy and Liberty, "This would be a good time to time-jump. Let's head away from the commotion."

As men and women crowded around the hatch and climbed

down to the tween deck, we mounted the now-visible Liberty and I said, "Back to modern day."

The last thing I heard before we jumped through the time portal was the captain yelling, "Francis Billington, if I ever see you with a musket on my ship again I'll strap you to the topmast and let the crows peck out your eyes!"

Chapter 6

Upon returning to the classroom we dismounted from Liberty. Tommy walked straight to the teacher's desk and grabbed his modern-day clothes. I asked, "So, Tommy, did you enjoy your adventure with the Pilgrims on the *Mayflower?*"

"Best. Detention. Ever!" he said. "I can't wait to go again."

"What do you think you'll remember the most?" I asked him.

"That's easy. I'll never forget the looks on the Pilgrims' faces when they saw land again. I mean they were so happy, they were crying. Even the men were crying. I know they were tough and put on brave faces, but when they finally saw the end of their journey it was like that rough exterior melted away."

"Real gratitude can do that to a person," I said. "Giving thanks with all our hearts is an emotional experience.

When we're truly grateful for something, we sometimes show it through tears of joy."

"I have a sister named Joy," said Liberty. "And she cried a lot, too, but not from gratitude. It's a long story but basically she was madly in love with this stallion and she thought he loved her, too, but then he left her for another mare and boy did the waterworks flow after that."

"I'm running to change my clothes," Tommy said. "I'll be right back." He ran to the door and slipped out.

I went to the teacher's desk, grabbed a piece of paper and a pencil, and wrote down some items that might be useful before we time-jumped back to the Pilgrims.

"I hope you're writing down a grocery list," said Liberty. "I believe I was promised a smorgasbord of fresh fruits and vegetables."

"Perhaps we should hang a feed sack to your neck so you have something to snack on twenty-four/seven," I said with sarcasm.

"Now you're talking," Liberty said with delight. "Oh, I almost forgot." Liberty walked over to the chalkboard, picked up a piece of chalk with his teeth, and then wrote on the chalkboard, "I will not throw wooden shoes through glass windows 100 times."

Tommy returned looking like a twenty-first-century boy again. He tossed me the traveling bag and I slipped it over my shoulder.

"Nice job, Liberty," Tommy laughed. "That looks like something I would do."

"Just trying to help out a . . ." Liberty gagged and then swallowed. "I think I just swallowed that piece of chalk."

"Well, I'm going to run over to the football field. I can probably catch the last half of practice," Tommy said. "Hey, I can bring this carp pie to my football coach. Maybe he'll forgive me for being late."

"Football, now *that* sounds interesting," Liberty said.

"Do you mind if we watch?" I said.

"Sure! We have a big game on Saturday. We're playing against our archrivals. But I also don't want to miss swordfighting with Captain Standish. That guy is cool. Do you think we'll be back in time for me to play in the game? It's so weird that I want to go to history class instead of football!"

"No worries, we'll be back. That is, if Liberty doesn't get lost wandering through a carrot patch searching for the perfect carrot," I said teasingly.

"No kidding," said Tommy. "Or he might wander into an Olive Garden for an all-you-can-eat special! I'm pretty sure the restaurant would lose money in that deal."

Liberty butted in and said, "Hello, I'm standing right here. And since when have I put my stomach before time-jumping?"

"Every time!" we said together.

As we slipped out the classroom door, Liberty held his breath and vanished. We walked down the hallway on our way to the outside door. Unexpectedly, Principal Sherman bounded around the corner and nearly tackled us.

"Mr. Revere," the principal said. "I hope Tommy behaved himself during detention." The principal raised his eyebrows as he looked at Tommy.

I couldn't tell if Liberty was close by or not. I looked at Tommy and then back at the principal and said, "I'm confident that Tommy learned a valuable lesson today."

"Oh, really?" questioned Principal Sherman. "Forgive my suspicion, but I've had other experiences with Tommy that have created a different belief. In fact, I'll even place a wager, a whole quarter for each item of history learned." He towered over Tommy like a monstrous wave threatening the *Mayflower*. "Anything, Tommy? Any tiny piece of information that might have slipped through to that brain of yours?"

"Hmm," Tommy replied. He glanced at me and I recognized that look. It was almost imperceptible, but I could see it. It's the same look that someone gives when playing chess just before saying "Checkmate."

"All I can say is Mr. Revere really knows his history," said Tommy. "You wouldn't believe all the stuff he had me do, I mean, learn. We started clear back in 1620 when the Pilgrims sailed from England to America. Did you know their voyage on the *Mayflower* took sixty-five days and more than three thousand miles? Almost everyone was seasick except for the sailors, who bullied the Pilgrims and teased them by calling them Puritans or Saints, but they were actually only half of the passengers. The other half were called Strangers, who were furious about not landing at the Hudson River and there was almost a mutiny but William Bradford saved the day with the Mayflower Compact that everyone signed which basically meant that they would stick together no matter what. Would you like me to go on?"

Principal Sherman's eyes were bulging. He was about to say something when the outside door at the end of the hallway opened; then a couple of seconds later it closed.

"Well, that's odd," I said, relieved that Liberty had gone undetected.

Tommy held out his hand to the principal and said, "That will be two dollars and seventy-five cents. Cash only, please."

The principal gave Tommy a half grin as he reached for his

wallet. "Impressive," the principal said, handing Tommy the money. "But I'm not falling for it. I don't know what kind of game you're playing, Tommy, but I'm on to you. Mr. Revere, if I were you I'd put eyes in the back of my head." And with that, the principal turned and lumbered down the hallway toward his office.

I smiled at Tommy. "Well said. Now, let's get you to your football practice."

We walked outside and saw Liberty waiting for us in the parking lot. We hurried over to him and climbed on. "Lead the way," I said. As Tommy guided Liberty to the football stadium I said, "Try and meet me and Liberty tomorrow before school. Come a half hour early and call or text Freedom to come as well. If you're up to it, we'll continue our journey with the Pilgrims."

"You bet! I haven't been this excited since Christmas morning," Tommy exclaimed.

Liberty laughed and said, "Except instead of opening Christmas presents, you'll be opening history!"

"You're right," Tommy said. "Who knew history could be so exciting!"

The next morning, Tommy and Freedom were waiting at the school by the time I showed up. "Good morning," I said cheerfully, dismounting from Liberty.

"Hi, Mr. Revere," said Tommy and Freedom.

"Tommy just told me about your journey yesterday. Well, most of it," said Freedom. She was wearing a faded yellow T-shirt and faded jeans. It was hard not to look at her black hair. It was silky smooth, as if she brushed it a thousand times. This morning there was a yellow feather clipped in it. "I'm excited to go with you today. I assume we'll be back before school starts."

"That's correct," I said. "After we're finished in the past we can time-jump back to the future, which, of course, is actually the present. In fact, we can only return within seconds of when we left. And we're unable to time-jump into the future."

Freedom pondered for a second and said, "So, Liberty can jump to America's past and return to our present but not its future."

"Correct," I said. "We've tried to jump to the future but the portal won't open unless we say the right words. *Rush, rush, rushing to history* has proven to be the most effective phrase."

Tommy said, "I told Freedom that today we're going to join the Pilgrims in America."

"First things first," I said. I pulled off my traveling bag from my shoulder and handed it to Tommy. "Your pilgrim clothes are inside. There's a dress for you, too, Freedom."

"It's a lot bulkier than yesterday," Tommy said.

"That's because you'll need some heavier clothing to help keep you warm. Liberty and I had to time-jump to the seventeenth century this morning to collect these."

"Is it supposed to be really cold? I'm a wimp when it comes to the snow," said Freedom.

"Yes, we'll probably experience freezing temperatures. We're heading back to the Pilgrims' first winter. Keep in mind that the Pilgrims landed in the New World and started building their first colony, Plymouth Plantation, in November."

"Anything else we should know before we go?" Tommy asked.

"If you get hungry I brought some additional snacks," I said. "This morning, Liberty ate enough for two horses."

Liberty snorted and said, "It's a well-known fact that breakfast is the most important meal of the day." Liberty paused for just a second and added, "Thank you, Freedom."

"Why are you thanking her? She didn't say anything," said Tommy.

"Yes, she did. She said that she supports my hearty appetite," Liberty replied.

"No, she didn't. I've been standing right here," Tommy argued.

I intervened. "It's apparent that Freedom has a gift. How long have you been able to communicate with animals?"

"Since I was about eight, I think," said Freedom. "My grandfather says that animals can feel what we feel, especially fear. Our emotions are powerful. He trained me to use emotions to speak to the mind of an animal."

"So, you're like a horse whisperer," Tommy said, smiling at her. "I'm good with that."

"Very well," I said, "run inside the school and change your clothes. Liberty and I will wait here."

Tommy and Freedom rushed inside the school and within a few minutes they were back outside dressed like Pilgrims.

"How do I look?" asked Freedom, spinning once in her green woolen dress. She also wore a white linen cap that came down over her ears, and a white apron. Finally, she wore a purple woolen shawl that covered her shoulders and hung down to her waist.

"Marvelous," Liberty said.

"I believe we're ready to go," I said.

"Will we join the Pilgrims right before they set foot on Cape Cod? Is that where Plymouth Rock is?" Tommy asked.

"Actually, no," I replied. "Plymouth Rock wasn't the first place the Pilgrims found. First, *Mayflower* anchored off the coast of Cape Cod at what is now Provincetown Harbor on November 11. It was so cold that a small search party left the *Mayflower*. They needed to first find a good place to build their town before everyone left the ship."

"Ugh, you keep mentioning the cold," Freedom sighed.

"I bet Myles Standish was part of the search party," said Tommy.

"Yes, he was. And so was William Bradford. In fact, William's journal said there were sixteen men who wore light armor and all carried swords and muskets. Can you imagine landing in a place you have never been to with nothing around that you recognize in the cold, cold months of winter?"

"Again, do you have to keep mentioning the cold?" Freedom said. She looked around nervously. "Anyway, I think we should leave sooner than later. The other students will start arriving soon and I'd rather not call attention to myself."

"Good point," Tommy said, scratching Liberty behind the ear. "Let's go. Are we going to land with the search party?"

"No," I said. "It took the search party several trips and many days of hiking in freezing temperatures. They searched all over Cape Cod and were even attacked by Indians."

"Seriously? You had to say *freezing temperatures*. Why don't we suck on ice cubes before we go," Freedom said. "We really don't have time for this conversation." Freedom searched left and right while fidgeting with her apron. "The school bus may have already arrived at the front of the school."

"Wait," Tommy said wide-eyed. "Did you say they were attacked by Indians? I thought the Indians were their friends. How many Pilgrims died?"

Elder William Brewster, Myles Standish, and other Pilgrims pray upon arrival.

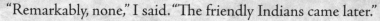

"Remarkably, none," I said. "The friendly Indians came later."

"I hope they had friendly horses, too," said Liberty.

"Not to make you suffer," I said to Freedom, "but I only mention the cold, freezing temperature because it may have been the biggest test for the Pilgrims. Think about it. How do you feel when you're freezing? And how would you survive with little food, few clothes, and really no idea where to go? These people were incredible! They had such a will to survive and thrive. Have you ever wanted something so badly you would work and fight and crawl to get it, even if you had to go through things that weren't very fun?"

"Oh, you mean like a house of mirrors?" Liberty asked.

We looked at Liberty in complete confusion.

"You know," he clarified, "the mirrors in the fun house at the carnival. Some people think it's fun to stand in front of them and see their bodies all warped and freakish, but I think it's terrifying. Except I had to do it! I had to go past those mirrors. It was the only way to get to the caramel apples!"

I sighed.

"That was very brave of you, Liberty," said Freedom, patting his side. "Now can we go?"

I finished by saying, "Finally, on December twentieth the Pilgrims settled on the location of their future home, which became Plymouth Plantation."

"Whoa," Tommy said, quickly doing the math in his head. "That means they searched for thirty-four days from the time they landed on Cape Cod to the time they started Plymouth Plantation. They must have been exhausted!"

"And *very* cold," I said.

"And *very* hungry," said Liberty.

"And I'm *very* ready to go," said Freedom.

"And I'm *very* embarrassed for all of you," said a voice from behind Freedom.

We all turned to face Elizabeth, who was already waiting with her smartphone. "Click."

Freedom looked mortified.

Elizabeth smiled and laughed. She was wearing a preppy blue and yellow checkered skirt and vest with a bright yellow bow in her hair. In one hand she was carrying a plate of pink frosted cupcakes. "I'm so glad I got to school a little early today," she said. "I'm bringing my favorite teachers a special treat."

"Thank you, Elizabeth," I said. "That's very kind of you."

Elizabeth gave me a fake frown, "Oh, I'm sorry, I said my *favorite* teachers. Not substitute teachers. My grade doesn't depend on you."

"Don't dis Mr. Revere," Tommy said. "He's an awesome teacher. And I better not see that picture on Facebook. I know where your locker is."

"No worries, Tommy," said Elizabeth. "I wasn't aiming for you. But I did get a great close-up of our poor little Pilgrim girl. And I really like your locker idea. We could post the picture on every locker! You know, in celebration of the Pilgrims."

Freedom sprang forward and tried to grab the phone. "Give me that," she said, as Elizabeth tried to back away.

Elizabeth pushed and Freedom pulled. Elizabeth may have been taller but she had a difficult time struggling with her phone in one hand and a plate of pink pastries in the other. As the two girls twisted and turned, I tried to step in to break things up. But before I could reach either of them Elizabeth's phone flipped up and away from her. As Freedom swung her arm up to catch the phone, she knocked the plate of cupcakes into Elizabeth's face.

"You imbecile!" screamed Elizabeth, wiping pink frosting off her forehead and cheeks. "Look what you've done!"

"I-I didn't mean to," Freedom stuttered.

Elizabeth frantically searched the ground. She squinted through the frosting until she spotted what she was looking for lying in the grass under Liberty. "My phone! Your freakish donkey better not step on it or—"

Crunch.

"Oops," said Liberty. He lifted his hoof but the phone was definitely crushed.

"You are in big trouble," Elizabeth huffed. "I'm telling Daddy." She spun around and stormed back the way she came.

"Now can we go?" asked Freedom. "Before her daddy comes looking for us. Her name is Sherman," Freedom said. "Elizabeth Sherman."

"Elizabeth Sherman?" I inquired. "As in Principal Sherman's daughter?"

"Yep, the very same," said Freedom.

Tommy walked over and picked up a cupcake from the ground. "This one doesn't look like it's been touched," he said, examining the edges. He peeled back the paper and took a big bite. "Izz weely ood," he said.

"Did he just say, *This wheel is hood?* Is that code for something?"

"Yes," Freedom said, "it means let's get out of here. I hear the bus!"

"Freedom, can you ride a horse?" I asked.

Instead of responding, Freedom sprinted and sprang up the side of Liberty and into his saddle.

"Tommy, you next," I said.

"I can't do that," Tommy complained.

"Aren't you the star quarterback?" Freedom teased.

"Yeah, but I'm not a ninja horse whisperer," he said.

Tommy walked over and I boosted him up.

"I'll jump through the time portal behind you, Liberty, let's go," I said.

"*Rush, rush, rushing to history!*" Liberty said.

As the portal opened and Liberty started to gallop I said, "December thirty-first, 1620, Plymouth Plantation, America." I watched Freedom and Tommy bounce on the back of Liberty as he jumped to our next history lesson. As I followed and jumped through the portal I instantly felt the freezing temperature on my face. Thermal underwear never felt so good!

We were at the edge of a forest. The trees were naked. Thin patches of snow rested on a thick layer of brown leaves like random quilt patches covering a blanket. I could hear voices and the distant sound of waves crashing on the beach. The sun was overhead but the weather prompted me to button my coat.

"Where are we?" asked Freedom.

"If we were in the modern day we would technically be in the state of Massachusetts," I said.

"Hey, when you guys talk I can see your breath," said Tommy.

Both Liberty and Tommy exhaled and watched their breath as it crystallized in the air.

"Look," said Freedom, pointing. "Are those the Pilgrims?"

Through the trees we could see a clearing. "Yes, those are definitely the Pilgrims," I said. "And I see a warm fire. Let's go over and see what we can learn."

"Okay, but first can Freedom and I take Liberty and ride to the top of that other hill?" Tommy pointed to a larger hill about fifty yards away. "I bet we could see Cape Cod from there," said Tommy.

"I'm fine with that. But you must stay with Liberty, no exceptions," I said, firmly. "Liberty, I trust you'll keep them safe."

"No worries, boss," said Liberty. "They don't call me 'Liberty the Dragon Slayer' for nothing."

As the three of them trotted away, I started my own course toward the Pilgrims. It was a cold but clear day. The small settlement was located on a flat hill. I saw several men carrying timber and others framing the side of a house. A few men were resting or chatting by a fire. I noticed William Bradford and Myles Standish speaking to each other as they pointed at different parts of the landscape. As I walked toward them I could see the *Mayflower* anchored in the harbor about one or two miles from us.

"We should be able to finish the Common House in about two weeks," said William as I approached from behind.

Myles turned and saw me first, "Rush Revere," he said. "We thought you were dead. Where have you been? Where's Tommy?"

"Indeed," said William as he rushed over and embraced me. "What a delightful surprise. I knew you were still alive. I wouldn't believe anything else. One passenger thought you had fallen overboard. But when we couldn't find Tommy I assumed that when we landed at Plymouth Rock and all the passengers disembarked from the ship, the two of you went exploring."

"That's exactly what we did," I said, relieved that William had assumed my alibi. "Yes, we, um, found a trail of sorts and decided to follow it. It was a foolish thing to do but I was strongly prompted to explore this New World."

"A prompting we have all felt, I'm sure," said William.

"Yes," agreed Myles, "but there is safety in numbers."

"All is well, Myles," said William. "And it appears that Rush Revere is capable of taking care of himself. But where is Tommy?"

"He and a new friend are exploring the top of that largest hill with my horse," I said, referencing the nearby hill.

"Did you say horse?" asked Myles.

"Oh, yes," I said, forgetting that neither William or Myles had ever met Liberty or Freedom. I had been thinking of a reasonable explanation and said, "As Tommy and I were exploring we became disoriented but were fortunate to come across a young Native American girl riding a horse. Strange, I know. But the girl took a liking to us and helped us find our way back to you!"

"No matter," said William. "The important thing is that you're here now."

"So this is your new home?" I asked, changing the subject. "How did you know where to start building?"

"It wasn't easy," said Myles.

"We have struggled, for sure," agreed William. "We searched all over Cape Cod. Some of us explored by foot and others explored using the shallop. Myles and his men survived an Indian attack."

"We have all survived hard things," said Myles. "William has had to survive the passing of his wife, Dorothy."

"Yes," said William softly. He sighed and said, "She died just before we found our new home. Her loss has been the hardest thing. But I also ache for many of our people who suffer because of the cold and lack of food. Many have the chills and cough and no place to get warm. But after thirty-four days since the *Mayflower* arrived at Cape Cod, we have found our home. This is Plymouth Plantation. Or it will be. For now, our people must stay on the *Mayflower*."

"It will make for a fine town," William went on. "When we arrived we found barren cornfields with the land strangely cleared for our homes. There is even a running brook with fresh water."

"Did someone once live here?" I asked.

"Perhaps," William said. "But we can see this place has been deserted for years."

"I heard you mention a 'common house.' What is that?" I asked.

William pointed to the frame on the ground and said, "This will be the Common House. It is one of the first buildings. It belongs to everyone. We've agreed to set aside our want of personal property or personal gain and instead create a community where the houses and buildings and profits belong to everyone. We are trying to create a fair and equal society."

I thought of the Pilgrims on the *Mayflower*. These were tough, strong, and independent people. I thought of them as self-reliant and ambitious. People who came to America to start a new life, build their own homes, work for themselves, and be free people. But what William Bradford was explaining to me seemed like the opposite. Certainly, it would be tempting to live in a society where everything is shared and all your choices are made for you. But is that freedom?

With some courage I asked William, "You say you're trying to create a fair and equal society. Do you think your people will find joy and happiness with this kind of common control?"

William sighed and said, "It will be a test, for sure. At first, the Common House seemed very attractive. This kind of control should guarantee our prosperity and success. But recently I'm beginning to doubt whether everyone will work their hardest on something that is not their own," William said.

"All these men are working on the same project," said Myles. "All week they've used axes and saws to fell trees and transport them to this site. The trunks will be woven together with branches and twigs and then cemented with clay and so forth. Some men do little and some men do a lot. When this house is finished, who deserves the benefit and blessing of having this roof over their head?"

I pondered the question. Was there a right answer? Certainly, no one should be left out in the cold. But at the same time, it didn't seem fair for everyone to be rewarded equally when people who were able to work chose not to. I finally said, "You're right. I think this will be a test. But I know you are both wise enough to figure it out."

"A fine answer, Rush Revere," said William, smiling. "Are you sure you don't want to be governor?"

"Not me. You'll make a fine governor," I said to William.

"If you'll excuse me," I said, "I'm going to track down Tommy and his friend and make sure they're okay."

"I think I can see your horse at the top of Fort Hill," said William as he squinted and looked over my shoulder. "We are building a platform at the top of the hill so we can mount our cannons."

"And soon we will build a fort," said Myles. "I'm sure Tommy will enjoy that."

"Ah, yes, there's nothing like building a fort," I said with pleasure. "I remember building forts in my living room with blankets and chairs. My brother used to always want to be the lookout. He would scream, 'Incoming!' and I would run around making sure all sides of our fort were secure."

"And did you have muskets and cannons?" Myles asked, smiling.

"Not exactly," I winked. "We had Nerf guns! They're very specialized weapons and highly effective in keeping out annoying little sisters."

Myles smiled, "Ah, these Nerf guns are good for little sisters but probably not so effective for savage Indians."

"Not so much," I said, smiling back at him.

Just then one of the Pilgrims working on the Common House called for William.

"Excuse me," said William as he stepped away from us.

"I promised Tommy I would teach him how to fight with a sword," Myles said. "However, it may need to wait until the spring, when it's warmer."

"No worries. I'll tell him and I'm sure he'll understand." I excused myself, again, and headed in the direction of Fort Hill. As I started climbing I heard the clomping of hooves and saw Liberty coming in my direction with Freedom and Tommy on his back.

"We saw Indians!" said Tommy.

"What? Where? How many?" I asked.

"There were only two scouts," Freedom responded. "They were

A re-creation of Plymouth Colony.

The Old Fort and First Meeting House, 1621, Plymouth Colony.

Pilgrims on way to church in mid-winter.

on a neighboring hill, watching us. They wore heavy pelts and furs. They were only curious."

"I'm glad you came straight back here. Good job, Liberty," I said.

"Did you find William Bradford?" Liberty asked.

"Yes, and I'm worried about their conditions, their health. They have little food and this weather is making life miserable for them."

"Let's give them our food," Tommy said. "Didn't you say you brought food or snacks? We don't need them."

"We don't?" asked Liberty, surprised. "I mean, what if we kept an apple and a couple of carrots and a—"

"Liberty!" said Tommy and Freedom in unison.

Liberty sighed, "All right. Sorry, sometimes my stomach takes me hostage."

I sighed and said, "I'm sure your parents would be very proud of you, but unfortunately there are laws to time-traveling and if we give these children a bag of fruits and vegetables it might very well save their lives."

"Is that a bad thing?" Tommy asked.

"No and yes. Your instinct of wanting to help someone is a good thing, of course. But we need to remember that we shouldn't change history. We should learn from it. Unfortunately, tragedy is a part of life. It's a part of history."

"But we could help one person, couldn't we? How could that really change the course of history?" asked Freedom.

"Look at it this way," I said. "Let's say we did help one or both of those girls. Let's say the food and clothing and medicine they receive could and probably would save their lives. Now let's say that one of those girls grows up and marries a cute boy in her town. The same boy who should've married another girl but because of our rescue effort, he never does. She never marries. The children she was supposed to have never happen. Friendships and families and futures are all gone because we helped one person to live when she was supposed to die."

"Does anyone have a tissue?" Liberty sniffled. "I don't know what's come over me. It must be my allergies."

"Okay, I see your point," said Freedom. "But I'm still sad to see them suffer."

"As well you should be," I said. "If we feel and learn nothing from the tragedies of the past, then we'll never know how to truly help avoid those same tragedies in the future. Certainly, we can't avoid all pain and suffering, but we can and should learn from it."

"I think I'm ready to go, Mr. Revere," said Freedom.

"Yeah, me too," said Tommy. "Can we travel to a time in history with less pain and suffering?"

I patted Liberty on the neck and said, "Liberty, it's time to spring forward to March sixteenth, 1620."

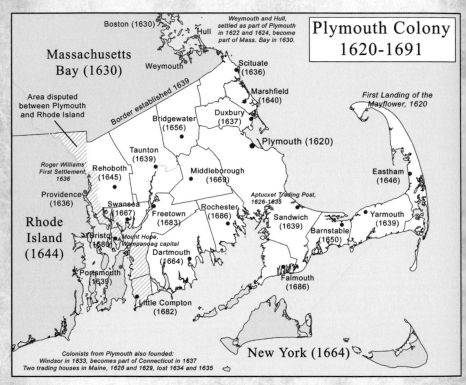

Eventually, the original Plymouth settlement grew into a thriving Plymouth Colony with thousands of Pilgrims.

Chapter 7

Birds chirped and flew among the branches of the many oaks, maples, chesnuts, hickories, and pines. The snow had melted and the temperature was at least thirty degrees warmer. About twenty yards away from us stood a deer, her short white tail twitching as she watched us between the trees.

"Can you talk to it?" Tommy asked Freedom.

"I don't think she understands English," Freedom joked. "But, yes, I can communicate with most animals."

"Helloooooooo," called Liberty. "We come as friends. Take us to your leader."

The deer just stood there, watching us curiously.

"Nope," Liberty said. "Nothing. I hope that deer isn't a member of the hospitality committee, because if she is I'm sending a complaint."

I watched Freedom as she stared intently at the deer. Its tail stopped twitching and it began to walk toward us.

Soon the deer was only a couple feet away, and Freedom walked over and stroked the side of its neck.

"You're more than a horse whisperer," Tommy said.

"No kidding," Liberty said. "You're like that girl who calls all her animal friends to help clean the dwarves' cottage. I hope we don't run into a witch with a poison apple. That would be bad."

"Check out all these tree stumps," Tommy said.

"What do you think they did with all these trees?" asked Freedom.

"I'm guessing they built houses," said Tommy. "I mean, I'm pretty sure after they landed in the New World they didn't check in at a Holiday Inn. There wasn't anything here! I mean, they basically were camping for months!"

"Good point," said Freedom. "When I hunt or track animals with my grandfather we camp for a couple of days but then we get to go home."

Tommy continued: "I used to go camping with my friend's dad all the time. He'd make us go really far and deep into the woods, and then we'd pitch our tent. My friend's mom hated it! She used to complain about not being able to plug in her hair dryer or take a shower. That was after one day! I can't imagine what she'd be like after landing in the New World with the Pilgrims. Ha!"

Liberty looked all around and said, "Come to think of it, it doesn't look like there's a drive-through for miles around."

"Nope," I said. "No McDonald's, no Taco Bell, no Kentucky Fried Chicken. Nothing. When the Pilgrims first landed they had to figure out everything from scratch. So what they did was basically try to re-create the town where they lived in Holland."

"That's really cool," said Tommy. "If I was building my own town from scratch I think I'd start with a football field."

"Seriously?" asked Freedom, rolling her eyes. "Before building a house?"

"Okay, well, maybe after my house," Tommy said. "But that would be kind of cool for everyone to be able to hang out at the same place and have some entertainment! Of course, I would be the starting quarterback. Oh, and I would totally invite you, Freedom."

"Thanks," Freedom said. "But I'd for sure have built a house first, a warm house, with a big fireplace so I don't have to camp during the winter! After that, I'd want to build a stable for Liberty."

"Ah, thanks, Freedom, for thinking of me!" said Liberty. "And maybe one of those Jacuzzi tubs with the rotating jets to massage my back."

I ignored Liberty and said, "The Pilgrims kind of built a football field. Well, a large place for everyone to hang out or gather and meet, called a 'Common House.' It was the first thing they built."

"I can see several houses or buildings over there," said Freedom as she peered and pointed through the trees. "Is that the Common House?"

I tried to look where Freedom was pointing and said, "I honestly can't really tell from here."

"What are we waiting for?" said Tommy. "I have a swordfighting lesson to get to."

As we got closer, I could see a dirt street with a row of seven houses with thatched roofs. There were also four larger buildings. One of those must be the Common House. Seven houses didn't seem like nearly enough to house the 102 Pilgrims who arrived on the *Mayflower*. I wonder if some chose to build a

town somewhere else. That seemed unlikely since the Pilgrims signed the Mayflower Compact, so they all sort of decided to stick together! Actually, the Mayflower Compact was supposed to provide just and equal laws for everyone at Plymouth Plantation, the very place we were standing. I'd have to ask William Bradford when I saw him.

I noticed the *Mayflower* was still anchored in Plymouth Harbor. Many Pilgrims, mostly men, were doing various chores: chopping wood, mending roofs, tilling a field for a future garden. A teenage girl was dipping a bucket into a nearby brook. Another girl was reading a book to a small group of younger boys and girls under a big oak tree.

"Let's go see if anyone is home," I said. "I'm especially curious why there are only seven houses."

We approached the first house and found a teenage boy carving a piece of wood with a long knife. He was sitting on a chair that looked too fancy to have been made in America. He saw us approaching and stopped carving.

"Hello there, young man," I said. "I'm Rush Revere. Do you live here?"

"Nah, I sleep across the way," he said. "I just like sitting in Governor Bradford's chair. He brought it from England. We don't have many chairs." He eyed Liberty. "Can I ride the horse?"

I looked at Liberty as he eyed the boy suspiciously. I turned back to the boy and asked, "What's your name?"

"Francis Billington," he said.

"Aren't you the kid who shot the musket on the *Mayflower* and nearly blew up the ship?" Tommy accused.

"You can't prove it," Francis said, standing up and putting the knife inside a sheath.

"Well, maybe it was your brother," Tommy replied.

"You can't prove that, either!" Francis exclaimed.

"Well, Francis, do you know how to ride a horse?" I asked.

"Any dimwit can ride a horse," he said. "I've ridden thousands of horses."

"Thousands?" I said, a bit surprised. "Well, then this one shouldn't be a problem for you."

Liberty shook his head and stomped his hoof.

"It looks like he's twitching to give someone a ride," I said, smiling.

"Good! I hope he's fast. I like going fast. Do you have a stick so I can make him go faster?"

Liberty backed up and huffed.

"You shouldn't hit a horse with a stick," Freedom said, stepping forward and petting Liberty on his face.

"You're just a girl. What do you know," said Francis.

Tommy started forward and I held him back.

"Very well, Francis," I said. "Let's see what you can do."

Liberty rolled his eyes and looked rather annoyed. I wasn't sure how this would play out but I thought the ride could serve a purpose.

I held Liberty's halter as Francis searched for a way to pull himself up into the saddle. He was a tall and wiry boy with curly brown hair. After a couple of unsuccessful attempts he finally managed to swing his leg over the saddle. He looked as comfortable as someone trying to water-ski for the first time.

He grabbed Liberty's reins and pulled left. Liberty didn't budge. He tried pulling to the right, but Liberty was immovable. I had never used a bit with Liberty and therefore he felt no pain every time Francis jerked the reins to the left or right.

"Stupid horse," Francis said. "Why won't he move? I've ridden mules that are smarter." It was the last thing he said on the back of Liberty because the very next second, the horse kicked up his hind legs and bucked Francis high into the air.

Francis yelled loud enough for all of New England to hear. He landed on the thatched roof of the house across from William Bradford's home, but only for a second, before the roof caved in and Francis fell with a thud.

"Francis Billington!" yelled a woman's voice. "How many times do I have to tell you to stop climbing where you don't belong?"

"You have to admit he had it coming," said Liberty.

"Look, there's William Bradford," said Tommy, pointing. "He's coming out of that larger building."

"Good eye, Tommy," I said. "Let's go say hi."

We walked along the row of houses toward the Common House. As we approached William I noticed how tired he looked. I didn't want to say anything, because that would be a little rude, but he really looked a lot older than when we last saw him, just a few months earlier. I couldn't really blame him. After all, he traveled across the entire ocean in a small boat under the hardest conditions, landed in a new place that was completely barren, and needed to build a town for all of the people who relied on his leadership. That makes me tired just thinking about it. Nevertheless, when William saw us he smiled and turned to meet us.

"Hello, Rush and Tommy! I've missed you! I assume you've been exploring, again?"

"Yes, we have," I said. "This New World is a bounteous land."

"It's a lot bigger than England," said Tommy. "I mean, it sure feels a lot bigger but that's probably because of the endless forests and unsettled land."

William agreed. "I only wish I could join you. But for now my duty is here at Plymouth Plantation. And this must be your new friend with the horse!"

"This is Freedom," I said. "We've spent the last couple of months teaching Freedom the English language. She's an exceptional learner." I hoped Freedom would play along.

"Freedom," said William, reverently. "I have to say I love that name. In fact, if I have a daughter someday I think Freedom would be a wonderful name."

"Thank you," said Freedom slowly. "Please excuse my grammar as I have only just learned to speak your language. I was born on the fourth of July, so my mother felt like it was the perfect name for a special day."

"Your English is marvelous. Does the fourth of July have a special meaning for your family?" asked William.

Freedom paused, realizing that the Pilgrims hadn't celebrated the Fourth of July yet. The Revolutionary War hadn't happened and the Declaration of Independence wouldn't be signed for another 156 years. It was only 1620 where we were, not 1776! She looked to me for an answer. As my mind raced for a way to help Freedom, we heard the sound of a loud bell.

"Either we're late for school or it's time for dinner," Tommy said.

"I hope dinner," Liberty whispered.

"Neither; that bell means Indians," said William, as he began searching the surrounding hills.

Pilgrims from every direction were heading for the Common

House. Women and children left their homes and men returned from the field and forest.

William pointed to a neighboring hill and shouted, "There! A single Indian on Watson Hill."

Sure enough, a lone Indian walked with long strides toward a brook that bordered the hill where the Pilgrim settlement was.

William spoke loudly so all within earshot could hear him. "Do not fire your muskets! The Indian walks boldly but he does not look hostile. He is only one and we are many. There is no need to fear. God is with us."

I was amazed watching this group of Pilgrims listen to William so closely. He was clearly the leader that they turned to for direction. Just like on the boat! They all put their muskets down and quietly watched.

Nobody else spoke as the Indian crossed the brook and began climbing the pathway up Cole's Hill. We were now close enough to see that he was a tall man. His hair was black and long but his face had no hair, unlike most of the Pilgrim men. However, the biggest difference was the fact that the Indian was practically naked. A piece of leather covered his waist but his legs and chest were bare.

"Hold your ground," William said firmly to his line of defense.

The women and children had gathered together farther behind us. I looked back and saw several holding Bibles. One mother covered her daughter's eyes and others had turned away from the approaching intruder.

Finally, when the Indian was only five yards from us he stopped, his path clearly blocked by the barricade of Pilgrims. His eyes were the color of tree bark. He had a large bow slung over one shoulder and a quiver of arrows over the other. Then he did something completely unexpected. He smiled and saluted us with much delight and said, "Welcome, Englishmen!"

"Wait, did he just speak English?" Tommy whispered. "How is that even possible? And he doesn't even look scared. He just walked up to us like it happens every day!"

"Shh, let's listen," I whispered back.

A gust of wind caught the back of the Indian's long black hair and it swayed up and over his shoulder. As he scanned the crowd of Pilgrims his eyes caught the movement of Freedom's silky black hair, which also waved in the wind. The Indian stared at her for just a moment, then turned to William Bradford and said, "Me, Somoset, friend to Englishmen."

William responded, "Welcome, Somoset. I am William Bradford, a leader of this colony we call Plymouth Plantation. How did you learn to speak English?"

"Me learn English from fishing men who come for cod." Somoset stretched out his arms and said, "This place, this . . ." He paused, pointing at the harbor.

"Are we playing charades?" whispered Liberty so no one else could hear. "Because if we are my guess is *harbor*."

I offered the suggestion to Somoset and said, "Harbor?"

"Yes," Somoset smiled, "this harbor called Patuxet."

Liberty whispered, "Am I good? Or am I good?"

Somoset continued: "Death come to this harbor. Great sickness. Much plague. Many Pokanokets die. No more to live here."

"You're saying that the Indians who lived in this area died of the plague?" asked William.

"Yes," said Somoset. "Many, many die. Much sadness. And you. Your people. Much die from cold and sickness. Massasoit knows. Waiting. Watching."

Visit of Samoset to Plymouth Colony, where he stated, "Welcome, Englishmen!"

William turned to Myles, then back to Somoset and said, "We come in peace. We only want freedom to live in peace. Who is Massasoit?"

"Massasoit great and powerful leader of this land. He watching you. He knows your people dying. He lives south and west in place called Pokanoket. Two-day journey."

"You must be hungry," William said. He saw Tommy and Freedom standing nearby and said, "Tommy, Freedom, run back to where the women are gathered and ask them for a plate of food and drink for our new friend."

"You got it," Tommy said as he and Freedom raced off to where the women and children were gathered.

William turned back to Somoset. "Please tell Massasoit that we come as friends. We are his friends. Yes, many of our people have died but we are strong."

Myles Standish clearly wasn't as quick to believe Somoset meant no harm. Since he was the main military man of the town, I can understand why! He probably felt he needed to defend and protect his people. Standish was wearing his helmet and breastplate. He firmly held his musket in both hands as if to say, Look here, don't make any false moves! His trademark sword was, as always, hanging at his waist.

Myles said, "Tell Massasoit that we have guns, bullets, armor, and powerful cannons. We are here to stay and we hope we can be friends."

"Together," said Somoset. "Massasoit and William Bradford, together."

"Yes," said William. "Together in peace."

Somoset smiled like he did when he first saluted us. "Me tell Massasoit. Bring Squanto. He speak better English. He help . . ."

Again, Somoset began gesturing with his hands, clearly trying to communicate the right word.

"Translate," whispered Liberty.

"Translate?" I repeated loudly to Somoset.

"Yes," said Somoset pointing at me.

William, Myles, Elder Brewster, and the rest of the Pilgrims looked impressed by my guesses. I turned back to Liberty and whispered, "You're making me look really good."

"I usually do," Liberty softly replied.

Standish, still not quite as welcoming as Bradford, said forcefully, "Who is Squanto?"

Somoset continued, "Squanto translate for Massasoit. Squanto speak like English man. Help Massasoit and William Bradford together in peace."

"We look forward to meeting Massasoit and Squanto," said William. "Will you bring them?"

"Yes, bring them. Return in five moons. But first, stay with William Bradford tonight. Need rest, food. Tomorrow, go to Pokanoket and Massasoit."

Tommy and Freedom returned with a plate of food and a flask and handed them to Samoset.

"Please, eat," said William.

Liberty whispered into my ear, "I can't believe he isn't scared! I'm scared just watching. It reminds me of a late-night movie I saw once. Well, I didn't see the whole movie because I was too scared. I mean if I were Somoset I think I'd wonder if my plate of food was poisoned. Or if I were the Pilgrims I'd wonder if Somoset wasn't secretly plotting to have all his friends sneak into the town in the middle of the night and—"

"You watch too many movies," I whispered back. "I'm guessing

William had a gut feeling. He relied so much on God's grace to protect them traveling across the rough waters for so many months, he just had to trust that this would be okay, too! It's really pretty amazing."

"Either that or Myles has a backup plan!" Liberty softly replied. "He doesn't seem to be joking around with that musket."

"Thank you," said Somoset. Before he took the plate from Freedom he reached out to touch the yellow feather in her hair.

Freedom handed him the plate of food and then reached up and unclipped the feather. She said, "A gift from us to you." Somoset leaned over and Freedom clipped the feather in his hair.

"A fine gift," said Somoset. Then he smelled the food with a curious look on his face.

William pointed to each food item, "This is a biscuit, butter, cheese, pudding, and roasted duck."

As Somoset used his hands to sample each item, William turned to us and whispered, "He seems like an honest fellow and eager to befriend us."

"Yes, but can we trust him to stay with us overnight?" asked Myles, suspiciously.

"Rush Revere, what do you think?" said William.

I cleared my throat and said, "Assuming he was sent to us by Massasoit, if we turn him away we may offend him, which may offend Massasoit. We can't afford to do that."

William turned to Elder Brewster, who said, "I agree. Our kindness may be our best ally."

"Yes, I agree," said William. "I propose we let him stay the night."

Liberty again whispered to me, "William really put you on the spot with that question. I couldn't have dug you out of that one.

Nice job answering him! Maybe you should get your own radio talk show. You know, callers call in with questions and you give them advice and stuff. I'd totally call you!"

We turned back to Somoset, who had finished the entire plate of food and was now drinking from the flask.

"Me like much," said Somoset.

"Come, Somoset. I would like to learn more about this harbor and anything else you can tell us about living here," William said.

This time Tommy leaned over and whispered, "Do you think Somoset really gives him the real scoop? Or do you think he'll hold back and wait for his next move like a game of chess? I mean he sure trusts William a lot without even knowing him! So, maybe he really does tell him everything he knows about this land."

I softly replied, "According to everything I've read, Somoset and especially Squanto became friends with William. I think they realized right away that they could help each other."

As the Pilgrim leaders led Somoset into the Common House, I decided this was a perfect opportunity to time-jump to our next destination.

"Guys, I don't know when or if we'll be eating with the Pilgrims," I said. "They seem pretty busy in there, so I suggest we time-travel to get a quick bite to eat, and then time-jump back in 'five moons' or five days when Somoset returns with Massasoit and Squanto. Liberty, did you catch that?"

"Uh, all I heard was blah, blah, blah, get a quick bite to eat, blah, blah, blah," said Liberty. "Was there anything else important?"

"I'm in," said Tommy. "All I had for breakfast was a stick of gum."

Homes and farmland surrounding Plymouth Colony.

"Is that what they call a breakfast of champions?" Freedom teased.

"What did you eat for breakfast?" Tommy asked Freedom.

"Are you kidding? I was too excited to eat," Freedom said.

"Then let's rush back to the present. Liberty? I imagine you're ready?" I asked.

"I was ready to eat when we got here," Liberty said.

Within minutes we found a secluded place just within the forest. When we jumped through the time portal we were standing in a parking lot behind a Dumpster with a sign that read PROPERTY OF FOSTERS' FAMILY DINER, FAST AND FRIENDLY SERVICE ON WHEELS. As we came out from behind the Dumpster we saw several old-fashioned cars parked in front of the diner. Waitresses with pink blouses, poodle skirts, and roller skates were taking orders and rolling back and forth between the diner and the cars. Liberty wasted no time and trotted up to an empty parking space. Freedom and Tommy were riding on Liberty as I followed from behind.

"You seem like you've been here before," said Freedom.

"Oh, I love a good fifties diner. And this place is especially good," said Liberty in a hushed voice.

I added, "No surprise we ended up here. This is Liberty's favorite place to eat."

Tommy asked, "So you can go and eat anywhere? Any time in history?"

"Any time in American history. However, I've tried to avoid bumping into myself. That could be problematic."

"So what do you recommend on the menu?" asked Tommy.

"Oh, I'm sure everything is good," said Liberty. "The menu has the usual hamburgers, hot dogs, fries, and shakes. But I always get the Veggie Supreme! With extra lettuce, pickles, toma-toes, cucumbers, spinach, sprouts, and guacamole on a sesame seed bun!"

"Guacamole?" asked Freedom. "Seriously?"

"Of course," smiled Liberty. "Everything tastes better with guacamole."

"I think everything tastes better with bacon," said Tommy.

"Well, sure, if you're a carnivore!" Liberty grunted. "I tried bacon once. I thought it tasted like dirty socks soaked in lard."

"You've actually tried dirty socks soaked in lard?" Freedom asked, skeptically.

"Blech! Gross! Who in their right mind would taste a dirty sock soaked in lard! That's disgusting," said Liberty.

Freedom complained, "But you just said—"

Freedom was cut off by the roller-skating waitress who asked for our orders. Freedom, Tommy, and I each ordered the cheese-burger, fries, and shake combo. And I ordered Liberty's usual, three Veggie Supremes, extra everything.

"Don't you think it's strange that she didn't ask why we're dressed like this?" Tommy asked.

"Not really. As I said, this isn't our first time here," I said with a wink.

As we ate our food Freedom said, "It's just really sad that the Pilgrims never had this kind of luxury. They never got to go to a diner and have food prepared for them in minutes. They had to shoot a duck or kill a pig or—"

"Or grow a garden," Liberty added between mouthfuls.

"What I'm saying is we have it easy," Freedom finished.

"True," Tommy said. "I'm pretty sure I would've starved."

I sighed. "Sadly, many of them did starve. In fact, that first winter was called the 'Starving Time.' When we met Somoset I counted the number of Pilgrims who were gathered outside. It was about half the number who arrived on the *Mayflower.*"

"Oh, that's what Somoset meant when he said that Massasoit knew that many of the Pilgrims had died, right?" asked Freedom.

"Correct," I said. "It was probably a combination of lack of food, the severe cold, and disease."

As the waitress rolled away after offering us each a free peppermint candy I said, "Why don't we all take a potty break before we head back."

"Good idea!" Tommy said. "The other luxury the Pilgrims didn't have is flushing toilets!"

Chapter 8

It was officially spring when we returned to Plymouth Plantation in the year 1621. To be exact, we arrived on March 22, five days after Somoset's initial visit to the Pilgrims. We landed near the top of Fort Hill, concealed by a number of trees and bushes.

As we were about to head downhill toward the settlement, I heard the sound of twigs snapping. I looked back to see what it was. Apparently, Freedom had heard the same thing.

"Did you hear that?" she asked.

"Yes," I said. "It sounded like it was coming from farther uphill."

"We're nearly at the top," Tommy said.

"Not farther uphill. It came from somewhere up in that tree," Freedom said, pointing to the large pine tree that rose more than one hundred feet in the air.

"I love those trees," said Tommy. "I'm ninety-nine

percent sure it's a white pine. Did you know that white pines can reach up to two hundred fifty feet in height and as much as five feet in diameter?" Tommy said.

"Who needs the Nature Channel when Tommy's around," said Liberty.

Tommy and Freedom dismounted from Liberty and we all walked closer to the trunk of the large pine. Just as we looked up, a pinecone fell from the interior branches and bonked Liberty on the nose.

"Ouch," said Liberty. "This forest is downright rude. First I get snubbed by a deer and then I get hit by a pinecone. I suggest we leave before we get tarred and feathered!"

Again we peered up into the branches. Sure enough, about thirty feet up was a man. No, a boy of about thirteen or fourteen. He looked tall and wiry and appeared to be climbing down the tree. Suddenly I recognized who it was and yelled, "Francis Billington!"

My call startled Francis and he lost his balance, slipping from the branch. In a split second I realized he was falling backward and away from us. My mind raced at the future implications. If Francis died because of the fall, it would be my fault. Francis was seconds from his death and I would be responsible for changing the course of history. I looked at Liberty, who saw my fear and despair, and suddenly everything on the hill that belonged to this moment in time had literally stopped. A bird had frozen in mid-flight just a few feet from Tommy's head. A squirrel was frozen in mid-scurry as it climbed a tree trunk. Even the twigs from a nearby birch tree were frozen in mid-bend from a recent gust of wind.

"Help Francis . . . quickly," Liberty struggled to say. His voice sounded strained, like he was holding back a locomotive with his mind.

"What's happening?" Freedom asked, a twinge of fear in her voice.

"This is freaky," said Tommy. "Mr. Revere, Francis is . . . he's frozen in time!"

True to his word, Francis hung in the air completely motionless, no strings attached. He was about fifteen feet above the ground that would very likely kill him upon impact.

Suddenly I had an idea. I ran to Liberty's saddlebag and opened it.

"Trying . . . not to . . . blink," Liberty said.

"Just a little more," I said. "Try and hold off time for another twenty seconds." I dug deeper into the corner of the saddlebag, "Found it!" I pulled out a mesh hammock that I had purchased when I thought I might be sleeping on the *Mayflower*. I ran toward the tree and called Freedom and Tommy to join me. "Quickly, you two hold the other end. We need to position ourselves directly under Francis and pull the hammock as tightly as possible."

"Eyes burning . . . bulging . . . twitching!" Liberty was panicked.

"Just a little more," I said.

Just as we finished stretching out the mesh beneath Francis, the air, the forest, the world suddenly came back to life, and Francis fell and landed dead center in the hammock. Thankfully, he wasn't dead. The hammock broke his fall as he slid off to the side and landed on his stomach.

I quickly gathered up the hammock as Tommy and Freedom helped Francis to his feet.

"I'm not dead," Francis said, brushing himself off. "That was a lucky fall. You know, if you hadn't scared me like that I wouldn't have fallen at all!"

"Are you sure you're okay?" I asked.

"I'm fine," Francis said. "You got to do a lot more than that to take out a Billington. That's what my dad always says. Out of twenty-two families who sailed on the *Mayflower*, he said we're one of the few who have all survived since landing in the New World."

You're still alive thanks to Liberty, I thought. *Liberty!* I turned and ran back to him. "You did it!" I said, rubbing his nose.

Liberty half smiled and weakly replied, "Yes, it worked. I actually stopped time for a few seconds. Although I'm still not sure how I did it. It was different than opening the time portal to the past or back to the present. That seems easy compared to this. This was different. It was like flipping a switch in my brain, although it wasn't really in my brain. It was more like a space between time. It was a place between the here and now. I'm sure that sounds completely ridiculous, but it's the best I can come up with right now."

"What else do you remember?" I asked. "Were you scared? Angry? Hungry? What were you feeling? And were you holding your breath or swishing your tail or crossing your eyes? I'm just trying to figure out if there's a pattern and if we could duplicate it."

"I don't think I want to do it again," Liberty replied. "It was exhausting. But I don't remember feeling scared or angry or hungry. Well, I'm always hungry, but you know what I mean. Mainly, I remember sensing danger and having the sudden resolve to do anything I could to help you."

"Courage," I said. "You were feeling courageous. Good. What else?"

"Hmm," Liberty pondered, "I remember keeping my eyes wide open like I was in the finals at the World Championship Staring Competition."

"I don't think there is such a competition," I said.

"Well, there should be, because I think I'd be really good at it!" Liberty sighed, "Anyway, when I finally blinked, everything went back to normal."

Francis finished brushing himself off and said, "I have to get back home. I need to tell the others!"

"Perhaps you shouldn't tell them about the fall," I said. "The important thing is that you're not hurt."

"Who cares about the fall," Francis said. "I'm talking about my discovery. I saw a giant lake of fresh water from the top of that tree!"

As Francis bolted down the hill, I stored the hammock back in Liberty's bag.

"No one's going to believe him," Tommy said. "I should know. There's no way Principal Sherman would believe me if I had some important news to share. I mean I know I goof off in class sometimes, but I'm an angel compared to that dude. And I can promise you that I will never shoot off a musket near a barrel of gunpowder."

"Good to know," I said, smiling. "But from what I know Francis Billington really did find a giant freshwater lake about two miles inland. Just like you said, William Bradford doesn't believe him at first. But, finally, Francis convinces the Pilgrims to scout it out and sure enough, they find it. And the fish and fowl that the lake provides becomes a huge blessing for the colony."

"Like I always say," Liberty yawned, "never believe a trouble-maker unless he's telling the truth."

We slowly headed down the hill toward the Pilgrims' settle-ment.

"I think I'm going to rest near that large oak tree," said Liberty. "I'm exhausted."

"I'm going to check out the brook," said Tommy. "Want to come, Freedom? Maybe you can talk some fish into letting me catch them."

"I'll come," said Freedom. "But I've never had any luck com-municating with fish."

"If you hear the bell, make sure you come straight back," I said.

As we separated, I headed over to the houses. As I ap-proached the first one, I noticed the door was open. Inside, Wil-liam Bradford sat in his chair with his elbows resting on a crude table. He had a quill pen in one hand and he looked to be writ-ing in a small notebook. He also looked to be in deep thought. For a minute I thought maybe I should leave, but I said to myself how often can you pop in and have a chat with one of your all-time heroes? I mean it's one thing to read about the Pilgrims and the leader of the first colony, and it's another to actually walk through his door and be able to ask him in person any intelligent question you could think of.

I softly knocked on the door.

William turned and said, "Rush Revere, you're always the last person I expect to see but it's always good to see you. Come in. Please, have a seat. I hope your travels have been kind to you?" He pointed to the oak chest sitting near his desk.

"Thank you," I said. "Yes, traveling and exploring have been good to me. I've learned much and hope to be able to share it someday with my history class." I looked around his modest home and noticed a fireplace took up one side of the room, a bed against another wall, and a Bible and silver drinking cup rested on his desk. His musket hung from pegs on the wall. I cleared my throat and said, "It's great to see the settlement growing."

"Yes, it's growing," said William, "but not as fast as it could."

"Why is that?" I asked. "Do you not have enough trees or supplies to build houses?"

"Well, no, not exactly. I can't remember if I told you while we were on the boat or not, but we have a contract with our sponsors in England, the ones who helped us pay for this voyage. The contract says that everything we produce or harvest, like food, furs, furniture, etc., must go into a common store and each member of the community is entitled to one common share. Eventually, we hope to make enough to pay back our sponsors in England. But I'm finding it difficult to get our people to work."

I pondered his comment and said, "So you're saying that everything that is produced, all the profits, go into, let's say, a box. And then everyone gets one equal share of what's in the box regardless of how much work they do or how much they produce."

"Correct," said William, "and some people figure that it doesn't matter how much they work because they're still going to get an equal share of what's in the box. I can't really blame them. I mean what is the incentive to work hard if you know the other person will get the same reward doing little to no work?"

"That doesn't seem very fair," I said. I thought about Tommy's football coach and the question he asked all the boys after practice. He said, "What would you think if two teams playing against each other get the same amount of points regardless of how many touchdowns they make?" The boys booed the coach, and Tommy asked, "What's the purpose of playing if nobody can win?" The coach replied, "Exactly! So get out there this Saturday and play hard! Play to win! There are a few of you who think you don't have to play hard to win a championship. Some of you think you deserve part of the trophy even though you're not giving your best effort. I'm here to tell you that if I see slackers out there, I'm cutting you from the team. And if you don't think that's fair, then you don't understand what it means be a champion!" Then the coach led them in the chant, "Play to win! Play to win! Play to win!" I then thought of the Pilgrims. They initially tried to make everyone winners but soon realized the attempt was failing because not everyone wanted to work hard enough to be champions. The truth is, when we try to make everyone a winner, no one's a winner.

William continued. "We thought people would be happy with a commonwealth, where no one owns property but rather shares what everyone else has. Instead, the idea is bringing much confusion and discontent."

To be clear, I asked, "If no one owns property, then you don't own your house or your garden or your business."

"Correct," William said. "I live here, but the house, the garden, or a business belongs to the community. And it has caused many of our people to do less instead of do more. We thought everyone working for each other would help the community flourish and prosper. But that hasn't been the case because men who work harder and smarter are beginning to wonder why they are putting all of their profits into a common box, as you say, so that other men who choose not to work receive an equal share of the profits. For the first time since the boat, I can see real tension developing! Anytime that I am in the Common House, at least three people come up to me to tell me they don't want to be doing all the work while their neighbor is sleeping! I'm beginning to wonder if the solution to our problems is for everybody to keep what they produce."

A knock came at the open door. "Sorry to interrupt," said Tommy. "Freedom and some other girls started braiding each other's hair and that's not really my thing. So I came to find you."

"Come in, Tommy," said William.

"I happened to overhear your conversation about how some people work harder and smarter but how others get all the perks. I'm not sure why but it reminded me of the county fair."

Tommy surprised me. I thought for sure he'd tell William about what his football coach said.

"I am familiar with fairs, since they have existed as far back as the Romans. But what is this 'county fair' you speak of, exactly?" asked William.

"Oh, well, it's sort of this competition," said Tommy. "People from all over come and see who has the biggest pumpkin or best pies or the largest pig. And the winner gets a cash prize like profits and a cool blue ribbon. People love it. They work really hard to try to have the best garden. They grow amazing vegetables like squash and cucumbers and tomatoes. My mom makes the best salsa and she enters it into the county fair every year and she's won three times!"

"Your mother makes salsa? I'm not familiar with this. Is that something that Somoset showed you?" asked William.

"Oh, no, but it's awesome. It's this great dip for chips! She chops up tomatoes and onions and chili pepper and a little bit of an herb called cilantro! My mouth is watering just thinking about it."

"I like this 'county fair' idea," said William. "Do you think we could have a county fair here in Plymouth?"

"Well, I'm not sure if you would call it a county fair, but you could use the idea if you like," said Tommy.

I looked at Tommy and smiled. I wanted him to know how very proud I was that Tommy was the one teaching!

"We could start by giving people their own plot of land to till, grow, and harvest their own crops on," William said. "Perhaps this could motivate people to work harder and be more creative with their skills, knowing that anything they produce would be theirs to keep. Perhaps a little competition could be healthy!"

I agreed. "Yes, it's quite brilliant! Those who work harder will likely produce more and then be rewarded more. Those who don't will not."

"Yes, I like it. I will consider this some more," said William. "Thank you, Rush. Thank you, Tommy. Our conversation has been very helpful. And next time we should try the 'salsa' you speak of."

The sound of footsteps made us turn toward the door as Freedom rushed in breathing hard. "Indians! Coming down the hill. About four or five."

A second later the bell starting to ring as we jumped up and ran outside.

This time, five Indians approached the settlement from Watson's Hill. As they drew near, I recognized that Somoset was leading them. I couldn't help but feel relieved. I imagine William Bradford and the other Pilgrims felt the same way. The Indians looked tall and strong. Each carried a bow and a quiver full of arrows and two carried several bundles of fur. Some were bare-chested and a couple had furs draped over their shoulders. The Indians stopped at the same place that Somoset had stopped during his first visit.

"Somoset return with Squanto," said Somoset, the yellow feather still clipped in his hair.

An Indian with knowing eyes stepped forward. He held a small bundle of animal skins and furs under one arm. He wore a necklace made of small seashells and his smile was bigger and brighter than Somoset's.

"I am Squanto," he said. "I used to live here in Patuxet Harbor. That was many years ago. I've been sent by Massasoit, the sachem and leader of this land. He permits me to come and speak with you. He will come soon. He is eager to meet you."

"Your English is extraordinary," said William. "How did you learn to speak the English tongue so well?"

"You must be William Bradford. May I call you William?"

"Yes, of course," William said.

The ease in which Squanto spoke English was unnerving. It didn't seem natural. And yet he was a perfect gentleman as he stood there in his leather loincloth and bare chest.

Squanto spoke again. "We have brought some furs to trade as well as some fresh herring to share with you. A small token of our friendship."

Myles Standish, who had also come out to meet the Indians, stood with his armor and musket and said, "When will Massasoit be here?"

"Before the sun sets," said Squanto. "He comes when he is ready. He could be watching us now. Every great sachem has eyes in all the forest. He watches. He waits. You are fortunate that he wishes to befriend you."

"We thank you for the herring," said William. "I'm sure they are delicious."

"They are not for eating," Squanto said. "They are for planting. If you're going to plant corn and grow a successful crop at Patuxet, you will need to fertilize the soil with these." Squanto held up the herring.

"Squanto know much. Smart. Listen to Squanto and live long," said Somoset. "Me leave now. Long journey home."

"Somoset is leaving with his men and returning to his people," said Squanto. "He is a sachem in the land northward."

Somoset nodded.

"But I will stay," said Squanto. "I will help you and do what I can to help Massasoit see that you are his friend and ally."

Somoset smiled and found Freedom among the Pilgrims. He walked up to her and held out his hand. Inside was a leather strap with what looked like a bear claw attached to it. "A gift for you," said Somoset.

Freedom accepted it and said, "A fine gift. Thank you."

Somoset gave one final look at the Pilgrims and then turned northward and left with his men.

Freedom turned to Squanto and asked, "You said you used to live here at Patuxet Harbor many years ago. Why did you and your people leave?"

"I have heard about the girl they call Freedom," said Squanto. "The girl with midnight hair who speaks perfect English."

"Thank you," blushed Freedom.

"Seven years ago, I was kidnapped and taken from Patuxet Harbor, never to see my family or loved ones again. I was put on

a ship and sailed across the ocean to a new world called Spain. Eventually, I sailed to England and learned to speak like you do. Finally, I had the chance to travel back to my homeland. I was eager to see my family, my parents and brother and sisters. But when I returned, there was nothing. Everyone was gone. I soon learned that the plague, a great sickness, had swept over Patuxet Harbor and killed my people. Hundreds and hundreds and hundreds . . ." Squanto stopped talking as he stared off into the harbor. He looked sad and distant.

"I'm sorry, Squanto," said Freedom.

"Yes," said William, "we are all sorry for your loss."

Squanto blinked and a tear rolled down his cheek. "You are kind. And you, too, have suffered great loss. Many of your people have died from sickness. This place has seen great sorrow for both Indian and Englishman. But I will try to change that. Together, we can learn from each other. Come, I will show you how to plant corn that will grow big and delicious."

Tommy nudged William and said, "Sounds like he could give you some nice tips on how to win a blue ribbon for best corn at the county fair!"

William smiled and said, "I like the way you think, Tommy."

As the Pilgrims followed Squanto, I called for Freedom and Tommy. "I think it's time we find Liberty and return to school."

"This has been a great field trip," said Freedom.

"No kidding. Do we get extra credit for this?" Tommy asked.

"Where did everyone go?" asked Liberty. "I had a nice nap over by that oak tree. Do you want to hear about the dream I had?"

"Sure," I said. "You can tell us all about it as we walk to some-place a little more private so we can time-jump back to school."

Tommy and Freedom climbed on the back of Liberty. And as

we walked into the forest to open the time portal, Liberty ended the day the only way a magical horse could.

Liberty said, "I dreamed that I was racing from town to town while carrying your revolutionary hero Paul Revere! Suddenly, a giant bolt of lightning struck the ground in front of me. I dodged it just as another hit the ground and then another. Each time, I barely avoided the bolts. It was like Zeus himself was determined to stop our midnight ride. Just before we reached the final town a lone food cart selling Veggie Supreme sandwiches rolled in front of us and I had to make a split-second decision on what to do. Should I stop and indulge myself with mouthwatering goodness or jump the cart and win the day?"

"What did you do?" Freedom asked with great curiosity. Tommy looked like he was equally interested.

"I don't know; that's when I woke up. I think an acorn hit me on the head. I'm telling you, this forest is out to get me!"

"I think you stopped for a midnight snack!" said Tommy.

"I think you jumped the food cart and saved the day!" said Freedom.

I pondered both answers and said, "You are a time-traveling horse that can stop time! So I think you did both!"

Facing page: Illustration depicting Native American Indian Squanto. He served as guide and interpreter for Pilgrim colonists at Plymouth Colony.

Chapter 9

The morning air was crisp but not cold as we dropped through the time portal and landed on the grass near the back door to Manchester Middle School. Tommy and Freedom didn't waste any time as they slid off the side of Liberty, grabbed their modern-day clothes, and rushed into the school to change.

Birds were chirping in the gnarled oak tree that shaded the back door. The sound of a large engine idling, like that of a garbage truck or a bus, was coming from in front of the school. It must be the school bus that Freedom heard right before we had time-jumped. As we peeked around the side of the school, I nearly stepped in a mess of pink frosting. Ah, yes, the incident with Elizabeth and her pink cupcakes. In a way, Elizabeth was like Massasoit. She was the leader or sachem of this school. Students either feared or revered her. She watched and waited for any sign of weakness in her classmates or any opportunity to send the message that she was in control. I wondered when our next meeting would be. And I wondered what happened in the meeting between the Pilgrims and Massasoit. I doubt Massasoit had brought pink cupcakes. But, hopefully, the two groups had better success at getting along.

Liberty watched the students exit the bus. "I've always wanted to ride inside a bus," he said, "but they simply don't make the seats big enough for extra-large mammals like me. I've seen horses ride in those fancy trailers and get pulled wherever they want to go. They probably get their hooves manicured, their manes permed, and their nose hairs plucked! No thank you!"

Tommy ran outside with the bulging travel bag and handed it to me. "Here are the Pilgrim clothes, mine and Freedom's. Oh, I almost forgot. Here's a letter from William Bradford."

I paused, not sure I heard Tommy correctly. "What is it? Who is it from?"

Slowly, Tommy repeated, "William Bradford, remember him?" He reached out his arm in my direction.

"Earth to Rush Revere, come in, Rush Revere," teased Liberty.

"Yes, yes, of course," I stammered, still trying to figure out how Tommy got a letter from William Bradford. "I'm here, I'm listening. You say it's a letter?"

"Well, actually, it's a sealed parchment, which I've always thought was cool because of the wax seal. Of course, the most common substance used to seal a letter was beeswax or resin. Did you know the pope would seal his documents with lead?"

Native American Indian sachem Massasoit visits the Pilgrims at Plymouth Colony around 1621.

"You're doing it again," said Liberty.

"Too much info?" Tommy asked.

"Oh, I don't mind," said Liberty. "I love the way your brain works."

"Yeah, but I probably sound like I should be wearing really thick glasses and a pocket protector full of pens. Anyway, here," Tommy said as he waved the sealed parchment in front of me.

I took it and examined both sides. Still a little confused I asked, "Exactly how did you get it?"

"After Squanto finished speaking and led the Pilgrims to the cornfield, William slipped this letter inside my coat pocket and asked me to give it to you. He said it was really important, but I forgot about it until I changed my clothes."

"Oh, well, that makes sense. For a second, I thought that William Bradford had figured out a way to teleport mail through a time-travel pony express service."

"Don't get any ideas," Liberty said, eyes narrowed.

"Well, I need to run and get my backpack out of my locker. Freedom already went to her English class. We'll see you in last period for Honors History!" Tommy waved and slipped back into the school.

"Well, what are you waiting for—open it up!" Liberty said, excitedly. "He said it was important! Maybe it's a treasure map! Or maybe it's the first clue to a scavenger hunt! Or maybe it's an invitation to his birthday party!"

I ignored Liberty as I pondered what William Bradford would send to me in a sealed parchment. I slipped my finger between the edge of the yellowed paper and the red seal until the seal broke. I opened the letter and read:

"Do you realize what this is?" I asked, excitedly. "This is an invitation to the very first Thanksgiving! What an honor!"

"I was hoping for a treasure map," said Liberty. "But the part that says 'lots of food' makes up for it. Let's hope they have a great harvest with lots of fresh vegetables! The invitation didn't say anything about what to wear, did it? I mean, I'd hate to come overdressed. I hope it's not formal. Tuxedos can be such a bother."

"Have you worn a tuxedo before?" I asked.

"Maybe I have and maybe I haven't. What's it to you?" Liberty said suspiciously.

I looked at the invitation again and said, "Lucky for you it doesn't mention what to wear, so that means you can come as you are."

Liberty smiled and let out a long, relaxed breath.

That's when I thought I would have a little fun with him. "Oh no," I said as I pretended to study the invitation.

"What is it?" Liberty asked.

"Well, I just noticed that your name isn't on the invitation."

"What!" Liberty snapped. "Let me see that!" I moved the parchment up to his eyes as he scanned the letter word for word.

I continued, trying not to smile. "That's too bad. I'm sure we could bring you back something. A carrot, perhaps."

Liberty's head jerked from the letter to my face. He gave me a penetrating stare as if trying to shoot laser beams from his eyes. His head jerked back to the letter. He stared some more. An idea must have popped into his head because he slowly turned to me with a big, wide, satisfied grin. He asked, "And just how do you think you're going to get to the Pilgrim Party, Professor? Hey,

I like that alliteration. *Pilgrim Party Professor.*" He refocused his attention and gave special emphasis each time he used the letter *p*. "The *point* I *prefer* to *punctuate* is that I'm your ride! You can't get there without me." Liberty smiled and blinked rapidly several times.

I couldn't help but smile and said, "*Perfectly played.* You're right. I'm sure it was just an oversight on William's part. We'd love for you to join us."

"Or perhaps the better way to say that is *I* would love for you to join *me*," Liberty said.

"Touché!" I laughed. As we walked away from the school I said, "Let's go gather some items for our history class as well as for the festival. Then we'll go have some lunch and return before class starts."

"Sounds like a plan!"

"But let's not eat too much. Remember, William said we should come hungry."

Liberty looked at me like he was embarrassed to know me and said, "You did not just say that. For the record, there are three subjects that have always put me at the top of the class: breakfast, lunch, and dinner."

We returned just seconds before the Honors History class started. Liberty, of course, held his breath and walked into the classroom unnoticed. I carried two large grocery sacks and set them down near the teacher's desk. As the bell rang and the students took their seats I reached up to feel the once-sealed letter from William Bradford resting in my pocket. I couldn't help but smile that we were invited to attend the first Thanksgiving.

I quickly welcomed the students and asked for everyone's

Dear Rush Revere,

The experience over the last several months is not something I want to repeat. I cringe at the thought of the many hardships I've endured: escaping from England, leaving my son in Holland, losing the Speedwell, sailing on the Mayflower, enduring miserable conditions overseas, feeling persecuted by Sailor and Stranger, suffering bitter cold and wretched hunger, and especially, losing my wife, Dorothy. The latter is something that nearly crushed me. However, I survived thanks to the friendship and the support of my friends in the New World. I consider you one of them. You always seem to show up at just the right time and at just the right place. I have struggled to know how to best repay you for your kindnesses. Although I know you expect nothing in return, I've decided to have a celebration of sorts. I feel the winds of change and good fortune are upon us. There is much to look forward to. Please accept this letter of invitation. The details are below. I hope to see you there.

Your true friend,

William Bradford

An Invitation
The First Annual Plimoth Plantation Harvest Festival
When: Late September or early October, 1621
Where: Cole's Hill (Plimoth Plantation)
Who: Rush Revere, Tommy, and Freedom
What: A celebration with games and lots of food
Come hungry!

Seal of the city of Plymouth, Massachusetts.

attention. As all heads turned in my direction, Liberty exhaled and appeared at the back of the classroom. Freedom noticed him but no one else did.

I noticed that all the desks were filled but one.

"Has anyone seen Elizabeth?" I asked.

Before anyone could respond, the door to the classroom jerked open and Elizabeth rushed in. She was so fast that Liberty didn't have time to disappear.

"Ah-ha! Caught you!" Elizabeth yelled, pointing. "See, I told you he had a horse in the classroom."

Principal Sherman was still inching his way through the door. Elizabeth quickly turned and impatiently pulled him into the classroom. In the two and a half seconds it took to look back and pull the principal through the door, Liberty vanished.

"What just . . . How did . . . Where did he go?" Elizabeth asked, confused.

Principal Sherman surveyed the scene.

"He was right there!" Elizabeth pointed as she marched to the back of the room. "Right here!" She spread out her arms as if showing off a masterpiece. She whipped around to the principal, who looked somewhat bothered.

Principal Sherman sighed and said, "I apologize for the intrusion. I always hate to interrupt a teacher's precious time nurturing the fine minds of Manchester Middle School. But Elizabeth was so passionate about it and assured me that you had a horse in your classroom. And not just any horse."

"That's right!" shouted Elizabeth. One of the yellow bows in her hair looked off-kilter. "*Daddy!* It's a talking horse who loves American history. He recited the Preamble to the Constitution.

He took Mr. Revere to visit the Pilgrims. You all saw it! And his horse really does talk! *Tell* him!"

Elizabeth stared at the students, urging them to back her up, but they all avoided her glare.

The principal walked to the back of the classroom and patted Elizabeth on the shoulder. "There, there, my dear. It's all right."

The students were all watching, eyes glued to the scene at the back of the classroom. In that exact moment, Liberty reappeared at the front of the classroom.

"There he is again!" Elizabeth pointed frantically to the front of the classroom. But, again, in the one and a half seconds it took the students to look where Elizabeth was pointing, Liberty had already gasped for air and had vanished again. I stood all alone at the front of the class and waved at all the searching eyes.

Freedom got up out of her chair and opened the back door. She said, "Is anyone else warm? This room feels really stuffy. I'll just leave the door open for a minute."

Smart girl, I thought. I hoped Liberty took the hint and was leaving the room.

"I think I'm partly to blame for Elizabeth's behavior," I said. "There was an accident this morning. . . . Oh, I almost forgot." I pulled out a new phone that I had purchased after lunch. "Here you go. And I do sincerely apologize about this morning."

"Accidents happen," said Principal Sherman. "Let's go to the nurse so you can lie down while I call your mother."

Elizabeth took the phone and started to squawk, "But *Daddy*!" Principal Sherman put his hands on her shoulders and started to leave. Elizabeth looked around the classroom one last time and then quietly exited with her father.

The whole class burst out laughing.

"All right, all right," I turned to the class and said, "enough of that. You all had an opportunity to turn me in, but you didn't. Why?"

"We like you!" said Tommy.

"Yeah, yesterday was awesome," said another boy in the front of the class.

"We hope Liberty comes back," said a girl sitting near the empty desk.

"We don't want to lose our talking horse!" said another boy.

"If that is how you truly feel, I can assure you, Liberty and I will be back. But we wasted enough time and we have an important history lesson today." I went to the chalkboard, grabbed a piece of chalk, and began writing some letters. K-I-S . . .

"Kissing?" guessed Tommy. The class laughed. "I thought this was history class." Then Tommy's face turned serious. "Wait, we're not going to talk about the history of kissing, are we?"

The boys all groaned, and the girls seemed very curious about where I was going with this.

"No," I said, "I'm not finished putting letters on the board." I continued writing,

K-I-S-T-I-N-G . . .

Tommy interrupted again, "Mr. Revere? It looks like you're trying to spell *kissing* and I'm no kissing expert, but I'm pretty sure you're spelling it wrong."

Again, laughter bounced off the classroom walls.

"Thank you, Tommy. But if you'll let me finish, I'll explain." I finished writing each letter. K-I-S-T-I-N-G-V-A-G-H-N. "There! Does anyone know what this says or means?"

All I got were blank stares. Timidly, a couple of students raised their arms.

"Is it some place in Europe?" said a boy.

"Is it somebody's last name?" asked a girl.

Tommy tried one last time and said, "I'm pretty sure it has something to do with a girl kissing a guy named Vaughn."

This time, I found myself laughing. "Imaginative, but no," I said. "Sometimes, what we see is not what is truly there. Most people see Liberty as an average horse. But you know differently. Likewise, most people don't see history for what it truly is. To know the truth about history, it needs to be experienced to be understood. When we begin to know the real people who were a part of real events in history, we begin to see those events differently. Today we are going to visit one of those events. Remember, oftentimes what we see is not what is truly there."

Using the same letters, I rearranged them and spelled T-H-A-N-K-S-G-I-V-I-N-G. "By simply unscrambling the letters, we see what is truly there. Tell me what you think about when you hear the word *Thanksgiving*."

"We get out of school!" said a boy in the back row.

"My family goes to my grandma's house and all our cousins come and it's like a big party," said a girl near the windows.

"I love watching football," said Tommy. "And my mom cooks a big turkey with stuffing. One year my dad tried cooking the turkey, but it didn't turn out so well and the fire department showed up, so, well, now he makes the mashed potatoes and gravy. And, of course, there's always pumpkin pie. I'm getting really hungry just talking about it."

The rest of the class agreed and starting talking about their favorite Thanksgiving foods.

I thanked everyone for their comments and said, "Today we're going to visit the first Thanksgiving. Of course, the Pilgrims didn't call it Thanksgiving. Their celebration was more of a harvest festival. Rather than try to explain it to you, I'd rather you experience it with your own eyes. History is a mystery until it is discovered. Are you ready?"

"Are you going to show us another movie? Do we get popcorn this time?" asked Tommy.

"Yes and yes!" I reached for the large grocery sacks and pulled out two large bags of popcorn, including some paper bowls. I also pulled out several packages of red licorice. The class cheered and several boys gave each other high fives.

"This movie is a documentary on the Pilgrims' first Thanksgiving. Pay attention to what's different and what's the same when you think about your own Thanksgiving." I walked to the back of the class and connected the wireless adapter to the projector. "I'm going to step out of the class to check on Liberty, but I expect you'll be on your best behavior. Enjoy the show." I dimmed the lights and discreetly nodded at Tommy and Freedom. As students were crawling over chairs and desks to get to the popcorn and licorice, nobody noticed the three of us slip out the back door. We hurried down the hall and through the doors to outside, where Liberty was waiting for us behind the gnarled oak tree.

"I have your Pilgrim clothes but you'll have to change when we get there. Liberty, try and get us just inside the forest."

Tommy and Freedom climbed up onto the saddle and Liberty wasted no time. "*Rush, rush, rushing to history,*" Liberty said.

"The fall of 1621, Plymouth Plantation, the first Thanksgiving," I said as I ran behind Liberty and jumped through the swirling time portal.

Chapter 10

I *immediately saw a* drastic change in the surrounding forest. Instead of the mostly green leaves of springtime, now the leaves were various shades of vibrant yellow, red, orange, and purple. It was definitely autumn and it felt like the perfect scenery for celebrating the first Thanksgiving.

Freedom and Tommy were experts at jumping off Liberty. They quickly slipped off their shoes and put their Pilgrim clothing on over their modern-day clothes.

"It feels like we were just here," said Freedom.

"We were," said Tommy. "Technically, we came here this morning. But about seven months have passed at Plymouth Plantation."

I pulled out my smartphone, tapped the camera app, and switched it to video mode. I turned the phone toward Liberty and said, "You're on. The students back in class will be able to see and hear you."

Liberty cleared his throat and said, "Hello, class. It's me, Liberty. I can't wait to get back and visit with all of you. Right now, we're approaching the place where the Pilgrims first settled in America. It's called Liberty's Landing."

"Liberty!" I whispered loudly.

"What?" Liberty whispered back.

"It's not called Liberty's Landing," I said. "You know that."

"I was just making sure you were paying attention. Although I do think 'Liberty's Landing' has a nice ring to it, don't you?"

I rolled my eyes and firmly said, "Get on with it."

"Okay, okay. We're approaching Plymouth Plantation. The Pilgrims have been living here for about ten months. And now a word from our sponsor."

"We don't have a sponsor," I said.

"We don't? Well, we should. The iced-tea factory that you work for should be sponsoring us. Seriously! Or what about Butterball turkeys! Or Stove Top stuffing! Or—"

"Liberty, I think I can take it from here," I said, exasperated.

"For the record, just because I'm a horse doesn't mean I don't have good ideas. Oh, I do. In fact, I have a dream. I have a dream that one day, I won't be judged by the color of my skin but by the content of my character! Wait a minute. That was brilliant! I could build upon that."

"It's brilliant because the Reverend Martin Luther King, Jr. said it first," I said.

"Oh," Liberty said. "It just goes to show how great minds think alike."

I turned the camera toward the Pilgrim settlement. "Class, this is Mr. Revere speaking. You can't see me because, as I mentioned before, the camera I'm using is attached to my coat disguised as a button. We are approaching the festival now!"

"Look at all the Indians," said Freedom.

Sure enough, I counted about a hundred Indians, double the number of English Pilgrims. I looked for William Bradford or Myles Standish or Elder Brewster but none of them could be found.

"Mr. Revere," Tommy said, softly. "I see a bunch of kids playing games over by the brook. We're going to check it out, okay?"

"Have fun," I said.

Tommy and Freedom ran off toward the brook and I started weaving my way through the guests. Finally, I saw a familiar face. Squanto was walking in my direction and waved as I approached. "You must be Rush Revere!" he said. "Welcome!"

"Thank you," I said as we shook hands.

"It is an honor to meet you," Squanto said. "William hoped you would come and bring Tommy and Freedom."

"We just arrived," I said as Liberty wandered toward the tables of food. "Tommy and Freedom ran off to see what games are being played by the brook."

"Smart children," Squanto said. "William recognized your horse and asked that I come find you. Come, he is with Massasoit. I will introduce you to the leader of the Pokanokets. As you can see, he has brought many of his people to the Harvest Festival."

I nodded and said, "It looks like he brought his entire village."

"Before I was captured and taken to Spain. I remember Massasoit had a great army. His people numbered almost twelve thousand, with three thousand warriors."

"That's remarkable," I said.

"Yes, but after years of disease, Massasoit was left with fewer than three hundred warriors."

I remembered Squanto talking about how many of his people died. I didn't realize how great a number that really was. I said, "I assume that Massasoit's visit with William Bradford and the others went well."

"Yes," Squanto nodded. "Very well. Massasoit and the people of the *Mayflower* worked out an agreement of peace. They promised to help and protect each other."

I liked the idea of a peace agreement. I was very glad to see the friendships that had been forged between the Pilgrims and the Pokanokets.

As I followed Squanto through the maze of people, I have to admit, I felt a little nervous and overwhelmed. I'm not usually starstruck, but walking around meeting exceptional people like Squanto, who left such a mark on American history, was just incredible! Not to mention, I was about to meet the man who could command his warriors to capture or kill the Pilgrims like the Indians did with the French sailors who had arrived in previous years. Instead, he chose to befriend them. And from the sound of it, the Pilgrims had helped the Indians as well.

As we approached several outdoor fires, I saw William Bradford standing next to a strong and muscular Native American. His chest was bare but he wore a thick necklace made of white shells. His long black hair was cut short on one side and his face was painted dark red. He had several warriors standing with him. Their faces were also painted, some red, some white, some yellow, and some black. William presented Massasoit with a pair of knives and some copper chains. In return, Massasoit presented William with some furs and a quiver full of arrows. The two men smiled upon trading the items.

Squanto turned to me and said, "Massasoit does not speak English, but I will translate for you." As Squanto approached the sachem, Massasoit turned and acknowledged him. The two spoke briefly and Squanto pointed in my direction. Both Massasoit and William turned and upon seeing me, William rushed over to greet me.

"Rush Revere, as always your timing is perfect. I see that Squanto has found you," William said. He took my arm and led me to Massasoit. "It is my pleasure to introduce you to the Indian king, Massasoit."

In his native tongue, Squanto translated for William and then introduced me to the king.

I reached out my hand toward Massasoit and he shook it with a strong grip. He looked to be about thirty-five years old and as lean and fit as any professional athlete. He smiled and spoke a language that was complete gibberish. I smiled back and nodded my head.

Squanto said, "He says that you have a strong name, like a rushing river."

Massasoit spoke again and Squanto said, "He asks if you have brought anything to trade."

I felt bad that I had nothing to trade with the Indian leader. Or did I? I slipped my hand into my pocket and pulled out the peppermint candy that was still there from our trip to Fosters' Family Diner. I said, "I have nothing to trade but I do have a small gift." I handed a piece of candy to Massasoit, who accepted it in his palm. He looked at it closely.

"Peppermint candy," I said. "You'll need to take off the wrapper, then place it on your tongue and suck it. It's sweet like honey."

Squanto translated my words and Massasoit placed the hard candy on his tongue. His eyebrows raised and he nodded at the warriors next to him. He smiled and spoke briefly as he continued to suck.

Squanto said, "He says your gift is good. He likes it very much."

Then Massasoit spit the candy into his palm and offered it to the warrior on his right, who took it and placed it on his tongue. One by one, the Indians surrounding Massasoit each took a turn sucking the candy and tasting the peppermint until it made its way back to the Pokanoket leader. Obviously, no one in the seventeenth century was familiar with germs or bacteria and how they can be passed along by the food we eat, the surfaces we touch, and even by the air we breathe. But they knew good candy when they tasted it!

William spoke. "Squanto, please tell Massasoit that our home is his home. And thank him, again, for the five deer that he brought to our celebration."

As Squanto translated, I turned to see the many deer, ducks, and wild turkeys that turned on wooden spits, roasting over the outdoor fires. Meats and vegetables were thrown into large metal pots similar to Dutch ovens and were simmering over hot coals.

"It smells delicious," I said.

"Squanto, Massasoit, if you'll excuse me. I'd like to show Rush Revere our settlement," said William.

Squanto translated and Massasoit nodded.

As William and I walked away, Squanto stepped alongside me and said, "I have a gift for Freedom. If it is acceptable to you, I would give it to her before she leaves."

"I think that would be wonderful," I said.

"Very good," Squanto nodded. "I will get it to her. Thank you, Rush Revere. You have been a good friend to William."

"And Squanto has been a good friend to me and our settlement," said William. "He taught us where to hunt and fish, how to plant and grow the best crops, what herbs to use for medicines, and how to trade for supplies with other tribes. We believe he's been sent from God as an instrument to help us grow and prosper."

"You are too kind, William," said Squanto. "God, as you say, rescued me from slavery in Spain. The Catholic friars, holy men, helped me escape. They risked their lives to free me so that I could return to my native land. I have much to be grateful for. And I choose to show my gratitude by serving my new friend and holy man, William Bradford."

I could see how Squanto would consider William to be holy. The Puritans prayed many times a day and they never worked on the Sabbath. They tried to show compassion to all men and women and looked for solutions to their problems without violence.

With great admiration I turned to William and said, "Mr. Bradford, I must thank you so much for inviting me. I am beyond honored."

William replied, "Tommy is a good lad. I wasn't sure if I

Map of private land in Plymouth Colony,
including the home of William Bradford.

would see you at the Common House, but I knew he would find a way to get my letter to you. I wanted you to be here to celebrate with us. We all have so much to be grateful for on this day."

"Yes," I agreed, "everyone seems so joyous, far different than a short while ago."

"It's true," said William. "But the real difference came when every family was assigned its own plot of land to work. That was the turning point! They were permitted to market their own crops and products. This had very good success. Men and women worked harder and much more corn was planted than otherwise would have been."

"The turnaround to success is truly extraordinary," I said. "And you say that it all happened soon after you stopped sharing the profits that gave every man a common share or equal amount?"

"Yes, at first we really had great expectations and high hopes that all the people would embrace the idea of a commonwealth. But it didn't work. In fact, it almost ruined us. We learned that it wasn't actually fair at all."

"But William is a smart man," said Squanto. "He gave people their own land. He made people free. No more slaves to a common house. They set up trading posts and exchanged goods with Indians."

William nodded and said, "In no time we found that we had more food than we could eat ourselves. We realized that our profits would soon allow us to pay back the people that sponsored our voyage to America. In fact, we expect more Puritans to arrive and surely more Europeans will come to trade with us."

I smiled at what William was saying. This, of course, is something that America has long since learned, but I marveled at how quickly the Pilgrims figured it out. When people have individual freedom to work, build, create, market, and make a profit for themselves, the community prospers faster than it would when these freedoms aren't available to men and women. It was obvious that this first Thanksgiving wouldn't be possible if William Bradford hadn't boldly changed the way the Pilgrims worked and lived.

"If you'll excuse me," said Squanto. "I must check on Massasoit. And then I will find Freedom and give her my gift."

"Again, it's a great honor to meet you," I said.

We said goodbye and Squanto slipped back into the crowd at the exact same time as Myles Standish walked up to us. He said, "He'll make a fine military man."

"Excuse me?" I asked, confused.

"Your boy, Tommy," said Myles. "I found him by the brook. He's quick as a snake and light on his feet. I was very impressed. He's a natural. I hope you don't mind that I gave him a gift."

"A gift? I'm sure he was thrilled to get a gift from you," I said.

"Indeed he was! He said his mother might be worried and I told him, 'Nonsense!' He should wear it proudly, day and night."

"Thank you, Myles," I said. "And, um, exactly what was it that you gave . . ."

My words were drowned out by the sudden sound of pounding drums and the loud shrieks coming from near the outside fires. I turned to see Indians dancing around a fire ring, their faces streaked with paint. Both Indians and Pilgrims smiled as they watched the performing Pokanokets twirl and bend and wave their arms as they sang and chanted to the drums. After several minutes the mesmerizing dancers finally stopped and several Indians whooped and hollered for more.

I turned toward William, who handed me a plate of food. "I'm sure you haven't had time to eat yet," he said. "Myles won't be joining us. As you may know, he, too, lost his wife last winter and is eager to find someone to marry. He fancies a young lady and has gone to court her. Please, sit, join me."

I thanked him and took my plate, which was loaded with food, including sliced turkey, a stew of meat and vegetables, and bread pudding. We ate until my belt felt like it was two sizes too small.

"Come," said William. "We will walk off this fine meal. I have something I want to show you."

We walked along the row of houses toward the harbor. When we reached the shore at Plymouth Bay we walked south along the sandy beach and then followed a trail that led slightly uphill toward a giant granite boulder the size of a large elephant. We climbed until the ground was level with the boulder, which stuck out of the side of the hill and into the ocean. My natural instinct was to step onto the rock and look out over the shoreline. The breeze was cool to my face. The waves were soothing as they rocked back and forth along the beach. Sandpipers pecked for sand crabs just before running from the approaching waves.

"You are standing on Plymouth Rock," said William. "We used this rock to guide the *Mayflower* back to this place after we found it on one of our discovery expeditions."

I had heard of Plymouth Rock since I was a little boy. I imagined a shallop or small boat could have used this rock at half tide as a dock for the Pilgrims to step onto dry ground rather than wading through frigid waters.

"I have tried to be like this granite boulder, steadfast and immovable," said William. "It has not been easy. But God has made the impossible possible. The Bible says we should build our house upon the rock. I have thought about this since we arrived. I have thought about this through each of our trials in the New World. Though the winds may blow and the storms may rage, the rock does not cower in fear. Do you know why?"

I waited for William's response, eager to know the answer.

He continued, "It is fearless because it knows where it belongs."

I paused before I said, "And you know that the Pilgrims belong here at Plymouth Bay."

"Yes," William said, nodding. "And each of us can be fearless and strong like this rock when we know, without a doubt, where we belong and what we should do. God helps us to know these things. I knew we would make it to the New World. I knew we would find a home like Plymouth Plantation. I knew, eventually, that I would need to give each family their own piece of land and allow them the freedoms to enjoy the profits of their labor. And I know, today, that this land will prosper and become a great nation. And it will remain a great nation as long as we are one nation under God."

"Thank you, William," I said. "I have treasured our time together and I will do my best as a history teacher to make sure that people across America never forget you or the Pilgrims."

Before we turned back toward the festival, I slipped out my phone and discreetly took a picture while William was distracted by several seals playing in the harbor below.

When we arrived back at the first Thanksgiving I said, "Thank you, again, William. I wish you the very best in everything you do."

"The same to you," said William.

He clasped my shoulder and we embraced. We said goodbye and I decided to head over to the brook to find Tommy and Freedom.

Several children were playing a variety of games like keepaway and leapfrog and hide-and-seek. Some Pilgrim children were playing tic-tac-toe in the dirt. Another pair was playing checkers with an old, water-damaged checkerboard and two different-colored stones. Finally, I saw two children sitting on tree stumps and in between them on a third stump was a very pristine but old-looking chessboard with elaborately carved chess pieces. Oddly, one was a Pilgrim boy with a sword hanging from his belt and the other was an Indian girl with a deerskin dress trimmed with fur and matching moccasins. She also wore a necklace of shimmering shells and two hawklike feathers in her hair. An odd pair of chess opponents, I thought. Both had their heads down intently studying the chessboard.

The next second the girl moved her queen to its final resting place and said, "Checkmate."

The boy was motionless, apparently stunned.

As the girl raised her head I quickly stopped the video on my smartphone and asked, surprised, "Freedom, is that you?"

"Hi, Mr. Revere," said Freedom. "Is it time to go?"

"Where did you learn to play like that," said Tommy.

"Playing chess is a lot like tracking animals," said Freedom. "I hunted you. And you stepped right into my traps."

"Huh?" asked Tommy, completely bewildered. "Let's play again," he said, determined.

"Not now," I said. "We need to head back to the modern day. Has anyone seen Liberty? Oh, and by the way, where did you get the Indian dress?"

"It was a gift from Squanto," said Freedom. "We talked for a little while. He said I should be proud of who I am and that I shouldn't care what people think of me. He knows a lot."

I thought, I'm sure he does.

"Yeah, and Myles Standish gave me this awesome sword!" Tommy unsheathed it and sliced it through the air. "We practiced for like an hour. It was so fun!"

"I bet it was. But let's not do that when we get back to the classroom, okay?" I asked politely.

I jumped when whiskers tickled my ear and I heard, "I sure wish they had a livery here."

"What's a liberty?" Tommy asked.

"Not a liberty," said Liberty. "I said a livery. It's like a spa for horses."

"Oh, yeah, I thought you said liberty, not livery. Hey, that's sort of a tongue-twister," said Tommy. "Try and say 'livery liberty' ten times really fast!"

"Oh, that's easy," said Liberty. "Livery liberty, liverty libery, libery livery, oh, hogwash."

As we walked to the place in the forest where we first arrived, I told Tommy, Freedom, and Liberty about my conversation with William Bradford.

"That's awesome that you got to stand on Plymouth Rock!" Tommy said.

I looked back at Plymouth Plantation and marveled at what the Pilgrims had accomplished. These people accomplished the impossible. They survived the unthinkable. And they started a new way of living that would influence the making of the greatest country in the world. The Pilgrims taught us that religious freedom comes with a price. They paid it with their lives while others lost the people they loved the most. But their sacrifices would not be in vain. I would miss my time with William Bradford. He was an exceptional American and someone who truly made a difference in the making of the United States of America. Of course, he would never fully see how the Mayflower Compact influenced the future lawmakers who ultimately created the Constitution. But I was excited to return to class and review what we had learned with the other students.

"So where are we going to go on our next time-travel adventure, Mr. Revere?" asked Freedom.

"Eager to go already?" I asked.

"Absolutely!" said Tommy.

"I've decided to visit Liberty's hometown and home time," I said.

"Really?" asked Liberty, excitedly.

"It's time to experience the history of the events leading up to the signing of the Declaration of Independence."

"There's no place like home!" Liberty said. "Unless your home is in a country ruled by a ruthless king or sitting under a lightning storm or on top of an active volcano or in the path of stampeding elephants or on top of a termite farm or in the path of a falling comet or . . ."

Tommy, Freedom, and I simply smiled at each other as we listened to Liberty's endless list. My life has never been the same with a time-traveling horse, I thought. And I wouldn't have it any other way!

A Final Note from the Author

Can you imagine being on the *Mayflower,* crossing a wide-open ocean with crashing waves shaking the boat? What about landing in a place you have never been and needing to build everything in your town from scratch? The Pilgrims truly were an amazing group of people who risked everything in order to be free and live as they thought best.

William Bradford, Myles Standish, William Brewster, Squanto, and Samoset were all brave and courageous figures! These were ordinary people who accomplished extraordinary things. Our country's history is filled with just these kinds of people. Their stories are both unbelievable and fascinating! I am really looking forward to sharing more of that with you in future books.

My buddy, Rush Revere, and his horse, Liberty, can go anywhere in American history anytime they want. How cool is that? I really hope you join us all for the next great adventure!

Quick, who taught Tommy how to swordfight?

Acknowledgments

For years, people were telling me I should write another book. I would shrug them off, giving one excuse after the other. I just wasn't inspired to write more political commentary.

Then, in early 2013, my wife, Kathryn, suggested an entirely different idea. She reminded me how often I talked about the importance of young people learning the truth about American history. She knew my frustration with what many kids are learning today and suggested that I tell the amazing stories of our country's founding in an easy-to-understand way. This concept did excite me and changed my entire attitude about writing another book! Suffice it to say, Kathryn was indefatigable in shepherding the entire thing, creating, coordinating, and assembling all elements. Thank you, Kathryn, for being an exceptionally bright, talented, loyal, and wonderful person to share my life with.

After hearing about the idea, my good friend the late Vince Flynn put me in touch with Louise Burke at Simon & Schuster, who helped to bring this all to life. Thank you to Vince, Louise, and everyone at Simon & Schuster, especially Mitchell Ivers.

Thank you sincerely to Jonathan Adams Rogers for being an instrumental part from the very beginning. He spent long dedicated hours helping to develop this concept from infancy.

My sincere appreciation goes out to Christopher Schoebinger for providing considerable assistance with writing, editing, and reaching a younger demographic. Spero Mehallis worked closely with Chris Hiers to create tremendously impressive illustrations, allowing history to be told in a creative way.

My brother, David Limbaugh, is an unwavering source of support. He is there for me at all times in all endeavors, and I am extremely grateful.

Photo Credits

THE
**MASSACHUSETTS
COAST**

SCALE OF MILES

0   10   20

Ipswich

Gloucester   *Cape Ann*

Danvers

xington   Saugus   Salem

Medford   Malden   Lynn

mbridge   Charlestown

Boston

Roxbury

R. Dorchester

Quincy

Weymouth

Cape Cod

*First Anchorage of
the Mayflower*

CAPE COD

BAY

Plymouth

Taunton

ance

wansea

MT. HOPE

Tiverton

Portsmouth

ort

Buzzards Bay

ELIZABETH
IS.

CUTTYHUNK

MARTHAS
VINEYARD I.

MASSACHUSETTS

BAY

ATLANTIC OCEAN

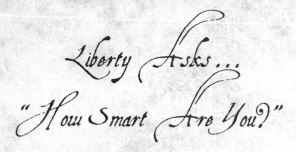

Liberty Asks...

"How Smart Are You?"

(Beware—He Thinks He Can Stump You!)

1. What was the name of the boat the Pilgrims used to cross over the wide Atlantic Ocean?
2. Where did the Pilgrims start their journey?
3. Where did Rush Revere, Tommy, and your favorite horse time-travel to first?
4. Who was the main leader on the boat?
5. Where did the Pilgrims land?
6. What color were my shoes in Holland?
7. What did we all say before we traveled back in time?
8. Who showed Tommy how to sword fight?
9. What did Squanto teach Freedom to do?
10. Who invited Rush Revere to the "First Thanksgiving"?
11. What was the name of the house where the town gathered?
12. Why did the Pilgrims brave the crashing waves to reach a new land? What were they searching for?
13. Were there any children on the boat? If so, who?

14. Were there any pets on the boat? Not including horses!
15. Who fell overboard? Not including Tommy!
16. In what state is modern Plymouth?
17. Who was the governor of the Plymouth colony when Rush Revere left?
18. What is the most misunderstood part of the "First Thanksgiving"?

Looking for answers?

Visit www.twoifbytea.com under Tea The People!